The Claim

THE ASHFORD LINE

A Western Family Legacy Saga

Book TWO

KADE VANCE

By KEVIN SENEY

Lucas Publishing - Lucas Media Company

Kalispell, Montana

Copyright © 2025 by Kevin Seney

All rights reserved. No part of this publication may be reproduced, distributed, or transmitted in any form or by any means, including photocopying, recording, or other electronic or mechanical methods, without the prior written permission of the publisher, except in the case of brief quotations embodied in critical reviews and certain other noncommercial uses permitted by copyright law.

Printed in the United States of America.

ISBN: 9798243756600

Lucas Publishing - Lucas Media Company

Kalispell, Montana

since 1899

www.LucasMediaCompany.com

Acknowledgments

Every story begins somewhere real. This one began with family—dinner conversations, road miles, long flights, quiet mornings, and the moments that never seem important until you realize they're the only ones that last. You are my fixed point—the place I measure distance from and always return to. Everything I know about loyalty, patience, and staying when it would be easier to go came from you long before it ever found its way onto a page.

Carrie—

Calm in motion. You see clearly without needing to be loud about it. The women in these books carry your steadiness not because I wrote it in, but because I live beside it. You make strength look ordinary—and that's the rarest kind.

Alicia and Jessica—

Raised in motion and still drawn to the horizon. One heals with precision, the other creates with style. Fiercely independent, beautifully self-directed, and completely unimpressed by the idea of settling. Watching you choose your own paths has been the best journey of all.

Emma, Katie, Gwynn, and Rachel—

I've been lucky to be your bonus dad for almost eight years. Your curiosity, creativity, and kindness show up here more often than you might realize. You remind me that imagination is inherited—and that love is something you practice every day.

Maggie and Aspen—

Our loyal German Shorthaired Pointers. You are the wind in our lives—the reminder to move, explore, and come home tired and happy. No better teachers exist.

With gratitude, pride, and all my love, **Dad**

Dedicated to my Grandfather:

C. Vance Lucas

*Some fires are meant to be passed,
not extinguished.*

Clarence Vance Lucas (1902–1983)

A steward of truth and a guardian of legacy, who understood that land, words, and family are not owned—they are held, and passed forward.

Found among the private papers of:

Clarence Vance Lucas

Undated. Written late in life...

*I did not inherit the fight.
I inherited what came after.*

*My father believed you could draw a line and hold it.
For a time, he was right.*

*After he was gone, I watched the world learn how to
cross lines without admitting they had moved them—
with contracts instead of rifles,
and inevitability instead of force.*

*They did not ask if the land should change.
Only how quickly.*

*What endured were not the loud victories,
but the quiet decisions— boundaries respected because
someone still remembered why.*

If you are reading this, the land is being tested again.

*Nothing is ever truly protected.
It is only held
by those willing to stay
when leaving would be easier.*

— C. Vance Lucas 1982

Chapter 1

ROUTINE REVIEW

(Book II — THE CLAIM)

The letter arrived without a return address.

No logo. No seal. No urgency.

Just a white envelope with her name typed cleanly across the front, the kind of font that suggested a government printer and a person who didn't think about stationery.

Carolyn Ashford opened it at the kitchen table, Wyoming light coming in flat through the east window. Morning had already passed its gentler stage. This was the working hour now—when trucks moved, gates opened, and people decided what kind of day it would be.

The letter was one page.

NOTICE OF COMPLIANCE REVIEW
Pursuant to County Ordinance 14.6.2(b), properties held under trust structures are subject to routine review to ensure continued alignment with land use, access, and environmental standards.

Routine.

Alignment.

Standards.

The words were arranged carefully, like furniture in a room meant to look neutral. No threats. No deadlines in bold. Just a date at the bottom—three weeks out—and a signature block that didn't include a name.

Only a title.

Deputy Administrator, Land & Access.

Carolyn folded the letter once. Then again. Not because she needed to, but because she always folded paper when she decided something mattered.

Outside, Mason Tate's truck was already parked by the barn. He didn't knock anymore. He never had, really. He came in through the side door like someone who'd earned the right not to announce himself.

"You get something?" he asked.

She set the letter on the table and slid it toward him.

He read it standing. Didn't sit. Didn't rush.

When he finished, he nodded once.

"That didn't take long."

"No," Carolyn said. "It didn't."

Mason folded the paper the same way she had, muscle memory mirroring instinct.

"They're calling it routine," he said.

"They would," she replied.

He leaned back against the counter, arms crossed, eyes on the window instead of her.

"Routine is how they test fences," he said. "Not to see if they hold. To see who answers."

Carolyn poured coffee she didn't need. The motion mattered more than the drink.

"Who's assigned?" she asked.

"Doesn't say," Mason replied. "That's on purpose."

She nodded. Silence settled—not awkward, just full. Wyoming silence. The kind that meant something was already moving.

A truck engine cut through it.

Not Mason's. Not anyone they knew.

Carolyn looked out the window.

A county vehicle rolled up the drive and stopped short of the gate. White. Clean. The seal on the door small enough to be polite.

The man who stepped out wore boots that hadn't seen dirt and a jacket that still creased where it should. He waited by the gate. Didn't open it.

Didn't ask permission.

He checked his watch.

Mason smiled once, without humor.

"Well," he said. "That's efficient."

Carolyn set the mug down untouched.

She didn't hurry.

She didn't wave.

She walked out onto the porch and stopped where the boards ended and the land began. The man looked up then—surprised she'd come herself.

"Ms. Ashford?" he called.

She didn't answer right away.

She let him stand there with the gate between them, the hinge rusted just enough to remind anyone paying attention that it wasn't decorative.

"Yes," she said finally.

He held up a clipboard—not as a threat, not as an offering. Just something he expected to be seen.

"County Land & Access," he said. "Routine review. I'm early."

"I noticed," Carolyn replied.

He smiled, quick and professional.

"Won't take long."

Behind her, Mason didn't move.

From farther down the drive, another truck slowed. Someone watching without stopping.

The man glanced past her, taking in the barn, the fencing, the way the land rolled without apology.

"This is just procedural," he said. "No action required today. Just observations."

Carolyn nodded.

"Observations go both ways," she said.

That gave him pause. Just a half-second. Enough.

"I'll need access," he said.

She stepped aside—but not toward the gate.

"You can stay right there," she said. "Tell me what you're observing."

He looked at the gate. Then back at her.

"That's... not usually how we—"

"I know," she said.

The wind moved through the grass like it always had. Unconcerned. Patient.

Somewhere, a line had been drawn once.

Now someone was standing on the wrong side of it, clipboard in hand, calling it routine.

Carolyn didn't raise her voice.

She didn't smile.

She just waited.

And the land did what it always did when someone mistook access for authority.

It held.

Chapter 2

ROUTINE

The first call came at 8:14 a.m.

Carolyn didn't answer it.

Not because she was avoiding anything—because she recognized the cadence. Early calls were never urgent. They were calibrations. Whoever was on the other end wanted to know whether she would make herself available before she knew why.

The voicemail arrived thirty seconds later.

Just checking in, the man said. *Routine questions. Nothing pressing.*

Routine always meant something.

She returned the call an hour later, from the kitchen table, coffee untouched.

"Ms. Ashford," the voice said, relieved but careful. "Thanks for getting back to me."

"Of course," Carolyn replied. "How can I help?"

A pause—small, but intentional.

"We're doing a general review of trust-adjacent holdings," he said. "Countywide. Standard housekeeping."

Housekeeping.

Carolyn wrote the word once on the legal pad beside her, then closed it.

"What prompted the review?" she asked.

"Oh, nothing in particular," he said. "It's just that when properties change hands, sometimes the paperwork lags behind reality."

"That hasn't happened here," she said.

"No, no," he replied quickly. "Of course not. This is just… routine."

There it was again.

She gave him nothing.

"If you need something specific," she said, "you can send it in writing."

Another pause. Longer this time.

"Certainly," he said. "We'll be in touch."

They disconnected without friction.

That mattered.

Later that morning, Carolyn walked the property line alone.

The land hadn't changed. It never did. The fence posts still leaned where they always had. Wind moved through the grass with the same disinterest it had shown for decades.

At the far end of the road, a truck slowed.

Not county.
Ranch.

The driver lifted a hand—half wave, half acknowledgment.

Carolyn returned it.

The truck didn't stop.

She stood there a moment longer than necessary, watching dust settle back into the road.

Nothing had happened.

That was the point.

By midday, Mason called.

"They reached out," he said. "County clerk. Said they're updating records."

"Yes," Carolyn replied. "They called it routine."

Mason exhaled through his nose.

"They always do at the beginning."

"At the beginning of what?" she asked.

"Of seeing whether someone moves," he said.

She looked back out the window.

"I didn't," she said.

"I know," Mason replied. "That's why I'm calling."

The email arrived just before evening.

Polite. Neutral. Formatted correctly.

Subject: Records Review — Trust Holdings

No accusation.
No demand.

Just a request for confirmation that everything already on file remained accurate.

Carolyn read it once, then again—not for content, but for tone.

They weren't challenging anything.

They were inventorying.

She forwarded it to Mason without comment.

Then she shut the laptop.

At dusk, she stepped outside again.

The air had cooled. Wind carried the smell of dry earth and distance. Somewhere beyond the property line, a gate closed—not loudly, just decisively.

She didn't turn toward the sound.

Routine wasn't pressure yet.

It was the clearing of a throat.

And everyone involved was listening for who spoke next.

Chapter 3

COLOR OF AUTHORITY

The second visit came with two vehicles.

That was the difference.

Not sirens. Not uniforms. Just the math of presence changing.

Carolyn saw them from the porch—white county truck first, then a darker SUV behind it, unmarked except for a small seal on the door that suggested cooperation without declaring it.

She didn't move right away.

Neither did they.

Engines idled. Wind crossed the pasture. The gate remained closed, exactly where it had been since the first visit.

Mason stood beside her, hands in his jacket pockets, eyes narrowed not at the trucks but at the way they were positioned—angled just enough to block the drive without fully claiming it.

"They learned something," he said.

"What?" Carolyn asked.

"They didn't come alone."

She nodded.

The man from before—Lott—stepped out first. Same boots. Same jacket. Same clipboard.

But this time, he wasn't leading.

The second man exited the SUV more slowly. Taller. Older. He wore a county badge clipped to his belt, half-covered by his coat like it wasn't meant to be displayed unless necessary.

He waited until Lott spoke.

"Ms. Ashford," Lott called. "Morning."

Carolyn walked to the edge of the porch and stopped where the boards ended.

"Good morning," she said.

Lott gestured behind him.

"This is Deputy Harris," he said. "Sheriff's Office. He's here as a courtesy."

Harris nodded once. Didn't smile.

"Ma'am," he said.

Carolyn acknowledged him, then looked back at Lott.

"A courtesy for what?" she asked.

Lott shifted his weight.

"For access," he said. "And safety."

Mason let out a breath through his nose—not a laugh, not quite.

"Safety from who?" he asked.

Lott ignored him.

"This is a multi-agency review," Lott continued. "We're authorized under county ordinance—"

"—to request," Carolyn said calmly.

Lott paused.

"Yes," he said. "To request."

Harris stepped forward then, just a half-step. Enough to change the air.

"Ms. Ashford," he said. "No one's here to cause trouble. We're just making sure everyone understands where things stand."

"And where do things stand?" Carolyn asked.

Harris glanced at Lott, then back at her.

"That depends," he said, "on jurisdiction."

Mason straightened slightly.

"There it is," he muttered.

Carolyn stayed still.

"Explain," she said.

Harris nodded, professional.

"This land," he said, "is held in trust. That complicates things."

"It clarifies things," Carolyn replied.

Harris didn't disagree outright.

"It changes *who* decides," he said. "County authority applies differently when land is structured the way yours is."

"And who decides that?" Carolyn asked.

Harris hesitated—just long enough.

"The county," he said.

Mason stepped forward one pace.

"That's interesting," he said. "Because last I checked, the trust charter didn't give the county standing on access."

Lott cleared his throat.

"This isn't about access," he said quickly. "This is about compliance."

"With what?" Carolyn asked.

Lott opened his clipboard, flipped to a page.

"Environmental standards," he said. "Survey alignment. Easement confirmation."

Carolyn listened without interrupting.

When he finished, she asked a single question.

"Which agency is in charge?" she said.

Lott looked to Harris.

Harris looked back at Lott.

The answer wasn't ready.

"That's what we're here to determine," Harris said finally.

Carolyn nodded once.

"So no one here has authority," she said. "Just interest."

Harris's jaw tightened—not angry, but alert.

"Ma'am," he said, "I'm here to keep this civil."

"It is civil," she replied. "That's why you're still at the gate."

Wind moved the grass again, patient as ever.

From down the road, another truck slowed. Didn't stop. Someone else counting.

Lott tried again.

"If we can just walk the line," he said. "Take a look. Ten minutes."

Carolyn didn't answer him.

She looked at Harris.

"Are you here under a warrant?" she asked.

Harris shook his head.

"No," he said.

"Are you here responding to a complaint?" she asked.

"No," he said again.

"Then you're here as a guest," she said. "And guests don't open gates."

Harris held her gaze. Measured her. Not as an adversary —but as something harder to classify.

"You're making this difficult," he said.

Carolyn nodded.

"That's usually how standing is tested," she said.

Silence stretched.

Finally, Harris stepped back.

"We'll note the refusal," he said.

"You can note whatever you like," Carolyn replied. "Just be accurate."

Lott scribbled something down, frustrated.

Harris turned toward the SUV, then paused.

"For what it's worth," he said, not unkindly, "this doesn't end here."

Carolyn met his eyes.

"I know," she said. "That's why I'm still standing."

Harris nodded once, then got back into the vehicle.

The engines started.

Dust lifted—not dramatic, just enough to mark passage.

When they were gone, Mason exhaled fully.

"That was a probe," he said. "Not a visit."

Carolyn watched the road until it emptied.

"They wanted confusion," she said.

"And?" Mason asked.

She turned back toward the house.

"They didn't get it," she said. "They just learned where it lives."

Chapter 4

STANDING

The trust meeting was held in the back room of the old feed store—not because it was private, but because it was familiar. Folding chairs. A scarred table. Coffee that tasted like it had been made out of habit, not hope.

Carolyn arrived early.

She always did.

The trust documents were laid out in front of her, squared to the edge of the table. She didn't reread them. She already knew what they said. What mattered now was who believed in them.

Mason came in next, carrying a legal pad he didn't plan to use.

"Anyone else here?" he asked.

"Not yet," Carolyn said.

"That's the problem," he replied.

They didn't speak again until the door opened.

First was Helen Cross—late fifties, rancher, hands that had learned patience the hard way. She nodded at Carolyn, warm but cautious, and took a seat without comment.

Then Eli Rourke, younger, restless, eyes already scanning the room like he was checking exits.

Two more followed. Quiet men. Good stewards. Not leaders.

Six seats filled.

One remained empty.

Mason noticed. Carolyn didn't look at it.

When the door finally opened again, it wasn't who they expected.

Tom Reaves stepped in—tie loosened, jacket still on like he hadn't decided whether to stay. He was the only one who worked mostly off the land now. Easements. Consulting. He knew how money moved even when it pretended not to.

He took the last chair.

"All right," Mason said, when no one else seemed inclined. "We're here."

Silence answered him.

Carolyn waited.

This meeting wasn't for her voice.

Eli broke first.

"I got a call," he said.

No one asked from who.

"They asked questions," he continued. "About access. About water. About timelines."

Helen looked at him.

"Who's 'they'?" she asked.

Eli shook his head.

"That's the thing," he said. "They didn't say. They didn't have to."

Tom leaned back, folding his arms.

"You're surprised?" he asked. "This is what happens when you stop being invisible."

Carolyn finally spoke.

"Invisible to who?" she asked.

Tom met her eyes.

"To people who assume," he said.

Helen frowned.

"They were polite," she said. "That's what bothers me."

Mason nodded.

"Polite means they expect you to move," he said.

Eli rubbed his hands together, restless.

"They mentioned fines," he said. "Not today. Just… hypothetically."

There it was.

The first crack.

Carolyn didn't react.

"Did they issue one?" she asked.

"No," Eli said. "But they explained how it works."

Tom smiled without humor.

"That's how they start," he said. "They explain."

Helen turned to Carolyn.

"You said this would protect us," she said. Not accusing. Just honest.

"It does," Carolyn replied. "But protection doesn't mean quiet."

Tom shifted.

"With respect," he said, "quiet is how some of us survive."

Carolyn nodded once.

"I know," she said.

The room settled again. Uneasy now.

Mason leaned forward.

"The trust didn't create this pressure," he said. "It revealed it."

Eli looked at him.

"That's not comforting," he said.

"No," Mason replied. "It's accurate."

Tom exhaled.

"I had a client once," he said. "Did everything right. Permits. Compliance. Cooperation. They still found a reason to make him sell."

Helen stiffened.

"Did he fight?" she asked.

Tom shook his head.

"He got tired," he said. "That's what they count on."

Carolyn folded her hands on the table.

"No one here is required to stay," she said. "That was never the deal."

Eli looked up quickly.

"You're saying we can leave," he said.

"I'm saying the trust doesn't trap anyone," she replied.

That landed heavier than resistance would have.

Tom studied her.

"And if someone does?" he asked. "If someone sells?"

Carolyn met his gaze.

"Then the trust adapts," she said. "It doesn't punish."

Helen let out a slow breath.

"That's easy to say when it's not your place," she said.

Carolyn nodded again.

"You're right," she said. "That's why it has to be your decision."

Silence followed—not awkward, but weighted.

Finally, Helen spoke again.

"My father used to say land doesn't leave," she said. "People do."

She looked around the room.

"I'm staying," she said.

One by one, the others nodded.

All except Eli.

He stared at the table.

"I don't know if I can afford this," he said quietly.

No one rushed to answer him.

Carolyn stood.

She gathered the papers, not to hide them—just to reset the room.

"This is what holding looks like," she said. "Not certainty. Not bravery. Just honesty about cost."

Eli swallowed.

"I need time," he said.

"You have it," Carolyn replied.

Tom leaned forward.

"And if the county escalates?" he asked.

Carolyn met his eyes.

"Then we respond," she said. "But not loudly."

Mason stood beside her.

"Noise is what they want," he said. "Process is what they use."

Tom nodded slowly.

"And conditioning?" he asked.

Carolyn didn't flinch.

"Only works," she said, "if you accept their timeline."

The meeting broke without ceremony.

No votes. No resolutions.

Just people leaving with more weight than they'd brought in.

When the room was empty, Mason remained.

"One hesitation," he said. "That's all it took."

Carolyn looked at the empty chair.

"That's how fractures begin," she said.

"And?" Mason asked.

She gathered the last of the papers.

"And fractures tell you where to reinforce," she said.

Outside, the afternoon had turned colder.

Wyoming didn't care who stayed.

But it remembered who tried.

Chapter 5

THE FIRST FINE

The notice didn't come by certified mail.

That was deliberate.

It arrived folded inside a plain envelope, postmarked locally, like a courtesy. The kind of thing that suggested familiarity rather than consequence.

Carolyn found it in the mailbox late afternoon, mixed in with seed catalogs and a handwritten note from a neighbor about a fence post that needed fixing.

She didn't open it right away.

She carried it inside, set it on the counter, and finished what she was doing. Fed the dogs. Rinsed a mug. Let the day complete itself.

Only then did she open the envelope.

NOTICE OF NON-COMPLIANCE — INITIAL FINDING
Pursuant to County Ordinance 14.6.2(b), the Ashford Trust property has been identified as requiring

corrective action related to access alignment documentation.

Initial.

Finding.

Documentation.

The fine amount was listed near the bottom.

$750.

Not enough to hurt. Not enough to matter.

Enough to exist.

Carolyn read the notice once, then again—not for meaning, but for tone. It was polite. It thanked her for cooperation that hadn't yet been given.

It included a deadline.

Thirty days.

Outside, a truck slowed as it passed the drive.

Not county. Someone else.

Mason arrived an hour later, the way he always did when something shifted. He didn't need a call.

"You get it?" he asked.

She handed him the paper.

He read it standing, then let out a breath that wasn't anger—just recognition.

"There it is," he said.

"Is it legitimate?" Carolyn asked.

Mason nodded.

"Clean," he said. "They didn't overreach. They didn't miscite. They didn't rush."

He tapped the amount with his finger.

"This isn't about money," he added.

"I know," she said.

Mason folded the paper carefully.

"This is a marker," he said. "First stone in the cairn."

Carolyn leaned against the counter.

"If I pay it," she said, "what happens?"

Mason didn't hesitate.

"Nothing," he said. "Which is the problem."

"And if I don't?" she asked.

He looked at her.

"Then the record changes," he said. "From cooperative to resistant."

Carolyn nodded.

Later that evening, her phone rang.

Not her cell.

The landline.

She hadn't given that number to anyone new.

"Carolyn Ashford," she said.

"Ms. Ashford," a woman's voice replied. Calm. Professional. Familiar without being friendly. "This is Raina Harlan, Deputy Administrator with County Land & Access."

Carolyn said nothing.

"I'm calling as a courtesy," Raina continued. "Regarding the initial finding issued today."

"I received it," Carolyn said.

"I assumed you would," Raina replied. "I wanted to clarify that this is not punitive."

Carolyn almost smiled.

"Then why issue a fine?" she asked.

There was a pause—not long enough to be a mistake.

"The fine is statutory," Raina said. "It establishes sequence."

"Sequence for what?" Carolyn asked.

"For resolution," Raina replied.

Carolyn waited.

"You'll find," Raina continued, "that addressing this promptly tends to simplify future interactions."

Carolyn leaned back against the counter, eyes on the window, on land that hadn't changed in a hundred years.

"And if I don't address it promptly?" she asked.

Raina's voice remained even.

"Then additional findings may follow," she said. "Larger ones."

Carolyn nodded, though Raina couldn't see it.

"Thank you for explaining," she said.

"You're welcome," Raina replied. "And Ms. Ashford—"

"Yes?" Carolyn said.

"This isn't personal," Raina said.

Carolyn paused before answering.

"I know," she said. "That's why it matters."

The line went dead.

Mason had listened from the doorway without intruding.

"She wants you to pay it," he said.

"She wants me to accept it," Carolyn replied.

He nodded.

"If you pay," he said, "you teach them you respond to sequence."

Carolyn picked up the notice again.

"And if I don't," she said, "I become a problem."

Mason met her eyes.

"You already are," he said gently. "The question is what kind."

Carolyn folded the paper once. Then again.

She didn't tear it.

She didn't file it.

She set it in a drawer with the trust documents—same place, same weight.

"I'm not paying it," she said.

Mason didn't smile.

"Then we need to be precise," he said.

"About what?" she asked.

"About why," he replied.

Later that night, an email arrived.

Not from the county.

From Tom Reaves.

Heard about the fine.
If this turns into escalation, I need to talk to my lender.
Just letting you know.

Carolyn read it once.

Fear had finally made itself useful.

She replied with one sentence.

I understand.

No justification. No reassurance.

Just acknowledgment.

Outside, the wind picked up, rattling the eaves—not violent, just persistent.

Somewhere, someone updated a file.

A $750 fine sat unpaid.

And for the first time, the record reflected what the land already knew:

This was no longer cooperation.

It was holding.

Chapter 6

THE SPLIT

The call didn't come to Carolyn first.

That was how she knew it mattered.

It came to Helen Cross, late morning, while she was fixing a gate hinge that had given up sometime during the night. She wiped her hands on her jeans before answering, already irritated at the interruption.

"Helen," the man said. "This is Mark Ellison, First State Ag."

She knew the voice. Friendly. Efficient. The kind that always called before problems had names.

"Yes," she said.

"I wanted to give you a heads-up," he continued. "Nothing urgent. Just informational."

Helen leaned against the fencepost.

"About what?" she asked.

There was a pause—not long, just careful.

"About your exposure," he said.

That word again.

"What exposure?" she asked.

Ellison cleared his throat.

"There's been a compliance action filed on the Ashford trust," he said. "Initial finding only. But once those things enter the system, they tend to ripple."

Helen felt the hinge go cold in her hand.

"My land isn't out of compliance," she said.

"No," Ellison agreed quickly. "And this isn't about enforcement. It's about risk profile."

She closed her eyes for a moment.

"What are you saying?" she asked.

"I'm saying," he replied, "that lenders don't love uncertainty. And right now, the trust is… visible."

Helen didn't answer.

"We're not changing terms," Ellison added. "Not today. But I'd encourage you to consider how long you want to be adjacent to a process that's still unfolding."

"Adjacent," Helen repeated.

Ellison didn't correct her.

After the call, Helen stood at the fence longer than necessary, watching the hinge like it might tell her something.

It didn't.

By afternoon, the shift had reached the others.

Eli Rourke got a letter from his insurer—routine policy review. No changes. Yet.

Tom Reaves received an email from a consultant he hadn't hired in years, asking if he'd "seen the corridor proposal yet."

No one said Carolyn's name.

They didn't have to.

The second trust meeting was smaller.

Carolyn noticed immediately.

"So did I," Mason said under his breath.

Helen sat down without meeting anyone's eyes.

Eli arrived late. Tom didn't come at all.

"Where's Tom?" Mason asked.

Helen hesitated.

"He had a meeting," she said.

"With who?" Mason asked.

Helen shook her head.

"He didn't say."

Carolyn waited until everyone was seated.

"This meeting isn't about the fine," she said. "It's about choice."

Eli shifted in his chair.

"I talked to my accountant," he said. "He thinks this could get... expensive."

"Eventually," Carolyn said.

"And until then?" Eli asked.

"Until then," she replied, "it's inconvenient."

Helen laughed softly—not humor. Release.

"Inconvenient is one word," she said. "My lender used another."

Carolyn looked at her.

"What did they say?" she asked.

Helen met her gaze.

"They said I should think about separating," she said. "Just in case."

No one spoke.

"That's how they do it," Mason said quietly. "They don't push. They suggest."

Eli leaned forward.

"I don't want to sell," he said. "But I can't afford to be the last one holding."

Carolyn nodded.

"That's honest," she said.

Helen swallowed.

"I said I was staying," she said. "And I meant it. But staying is starting to feel like… volunteering."

Carolyn didn't rush to answer.

She let the silence work.

"This trust was never a shield," she said finally. "It was a line. Lines don't protect you from pressure. They show you where it comes from."

Eli shook his head.

"That doesn't help me sleep," he said.

"No," Carolyn agreed. "It helps you decide."

Mason leaned forward.

"If someone wants out," he said, "there are mechanisms. Clean ones."

Helen looked at him.

"And if someone leaving weakens the rest?" she asked.

Mason didn't dodge it.

"Then the rest have to decide if they're holding land," he said, "or waiting to be bought."

That landed hard.

Eli stared at the table.

"I need time," he said again.

"You have it," Carolyn replied. "But not forever."

Helen looked up sharply.

"That's the first deadline you've mentioned," she said.

Carolyn nodded.

"Because this is the first decision that belongs to us," she said. "Not the county."

Silence returned—different now. Thinner.

Finally, Helen stood.

"I'm not leaving," she said. "Not yet. But I need to talk to my son."

Carolyn nodded.

"That's fair," she said.

Eli stood too.

"I'm not deciding today," he said.

"That's also fair," Carolyn replied.

When the meeting broke, only Mason remained.

"They're testing for yield," he said. "Not compliance."

Carolyn looked at the empty chairs.

"They found it," she said.

Mason frowned.

"Found what?"

"The seam," she replied. "Fear doesn't split evenly. It looks for weakness."

"And?" Mason asked.

Carolyn gathered the papers, steady.

"And now we know where they'll push next," she said.

Outside, a storm was building in the distance—not close enough to smell, not far enough to ignore.

Somewhere between staying and selling, the trust had changed.

Not broken.

Just stressed.

And stress, in Wyoming, always reveals structure.

Chapter 7

READING THE ANGLE

Kade Vance didn't come because of the fine.

He came because of the timing.

Carolyn hadn't asked him to intervene. She hadn't asked him for strategy. She'd asked one question, and it hadn't been framed like a problem.

Can you look at something?

That was all.

Kade arrived late afternoon, dust still hanging low over the drive. He parked where he always did—off to the side, wheels turned slightly out, habit from places where staying too long meant something else was coming.

He didn't bring a notebook.

He didn't bring a phone.

He brought time.

Carolyn met him on the porch. No greetings. No updates.

She handed him the folder.

Inside were copies—notice, fine, ordinance excerpt, a timeline Mason had written out in block letters.

Kade didn't read them right away.

He looked past her instead. At the gate. The fence line. The place where the county truck had stopped the first time.

"They didn't come all the way in," he said.

"No," Carolyn replied.

"That matters," he said.

He flipped open the folder then, scanning quickly—not reading words, reading sequence.

"How many agencies?" he asked.

"Two so far," she said. "Three, if you count lenders."

He nodded once.

"They always start with something that feels optional," he said. "If you comply early, they never have to show authority."

"And if you don't?" she asked.

"Then they escalate sideways," he said. "Not up."

Mason joined them, leaning against the railing.

"You saying this isn't enforcement?" Mason asked.

Kade shook his head.

"No," he said. "Enforcement is loud. This is conditioning."

Carolyn waited.

"They're teaching you a language," Kade continued. "Fines, reviews, site visits. Each one asks the same question."

"What question?" Mason asked.

Kade closed the folder.

How tired are you willing to get?

He didn't say it out loud.

He didn't have to.

Carolyn looked down the drive.

"They're not wrong about one thing," she said. "This will cost."

Kade nodded.

"Of course it will," he said. "If it didn't, they'd use something else."

Mason crossed his arms.

"So what do we do?" he asked.

Kade didn't answer right away.

He walked to the edge of the porch, stepped down, and stood where the boards ended and the land began—same place Carolyn had stood days earlier.

He looked back at them.

"You don't fight this by refusing everything," he said. "That makes you a story."

Carolyn watched him carefully.

"And you don't comply with everything," he continued. "That makes you a precedent."

Mason frowned.

"So where's the line?" he asked.

Kade smiled faintly.

"That's the trick," he said. "You don't draw it. You let *them* show you where it is."

Carolyn tilted her head.

"Explain," she said.

"They're moving in sequence," Kade said. "County first. Badge second. Paper third. Next comes something that requires you to respond publicly."

Mason stiffened.

"The fine?" he asked.

"No," Kade replied. "The appeal."

Carolyn looked at him sharply.

"They want you to contest," he said. "They want you to enter their process. Hearings. Records. Deadlines."

"And if I don't?" she asked.

Kade met her eyes.

"Then they escalate again," he said. "But every escalation costs them more than it costs you."

Mason shook his head.

"That doesn't feel true," he said.

Kade didn't argue.

"It doesn't feel true until you see the pattern," he said. "This isn't about land use. It's about tempo."

Carolyn folded her arms.

"They're setting the pace," she said.

"They're testing whether they can," Kade replied.

Silence settled.

Finally, Carolyn spoke.

"If I pay the fine," she said, "they win."

"Yes," Kade said.

"If I refuse," she said, "they escalate."

"Yes," he said again.

She studied him.

"And if I acknowledge it without contest?" she asked.

Kade smiled—not approval. Recognition.

"There it is," he said.

Mason looked between them.

"What does that look like?" he asked.

Kade answered carefully.

"You respond," he said. "But not inside their frame. You document receipt. You reserve rights. You don't appeal. You don't explain."

"And then?" Mason asked.

Kade looked down the drive again, as if the answer was already there.

"Then you wait," he said. "Because the next move tells you everything."

Carolyn nodded slowly.

"This isn't enforcement," she said.

"No," Kade agreed. "It's rehearsal."

"For what?" Mason asked.

Kade's voice stayed even.

"For conditioning landholders to move before they're told."

Carolyn exhaled.

"So we hold," she said.

Kade nodded.

"But not loudly," he said. "And not alone."

Mason raised an eyebrow.

"Who else?" he asked.

Kade glanced back at the house.

"Anyone who notices when language changes," he said. "And anyone who understands that legitimacy is a long game."

Carolyn looked at the folder again.

"And if someone in the trust breaks?" she asked.

Kade didn't soften it.

"Then the system learns something," he said. "And so do you."

The wind moved through the grass again, steady, indifferent.

Carolyn closed the folder.

"Then we don't rush," she said.

Kade nodded.

"Good," he said. "Because rushing is what they're hoping for."

He stepped back toward his truck, already finished.

"I'll stay close," he said. "But I won't lead."

Carolyn watched him go.

"That's new," Mason said.

Kade paused at the door.

"No," he said. "That's how this kind of thing always works."

He drove off without dust or drama.

Behind him, the land remained.

And for the first time since the notice arrived, Carolyn understood exactly what was being tested.

Not compliance.

Endurance.

Chapter 8

HOLDING

Carolyn did nothing.

That was the point.

She didn't issue a statement. She didn't call a reporter. She didn't ask anyone to intervene on her behalf. She didn't appeal the fine, didn't contest the notice, didn't explain her reasons to people who hadn't asked in good faith.

She documented receipt.

That was all.

A single letter, mailed back to the county within the window they'd allowed, written in neutral language and signed without flourish.

Receipt acknowledged.
Rights reserved.
No further comment at this time.

No argument.
No emotion.
No invitation.

Mason read it once, then again.

"They're going to hate this," he said.

Carolyn folded the copy and slid it into the file.

"Hate would mean reaction," she said. "This denies them that."

The days that followed were uneventful in ways that felt deliberate.

No trucks.
No follow-up notices.
No calls.

Just silence.

The fine remained unpaid. The deadline ticked closer without ceremony. County offices continued to operate as if nothing unusual was happening—which, in their world, was exactly how pressure matured.

Helen Cross called once.

"I talked to my son," she said. "He thinks I'm crazy."

Carolyn smiled faintly.

"Does that change anything?" she asked.

Helen exhaled.

"No," she said. "But it makes it lonelier."

Carolyn let that sit.

"Lonely doesn't mean wrong," she said.

Eli didn't call.

Tom sent a brief text instead.

Still in. For now.

Carolyn didn't respond. Acknowledgment wasn't required.

The county calendar rolled forward.

The deadline passed.

And still—nothing.

That was when the waiting became work.

Mason noticed it first.

"They're recalculating," he said one evening, watching the road from the porch.

"They expected noise," Carolyn replied. "Or retreat."

"And got neither," he said.

She nodded.

Kade checked in once, briefly.

Any movement?

No, she wrote back.

Good, came the reply.

On the thirty-third day after the fine had been issued, a new letter arrived.

Not a notice.

A memo.

Internal. Misdirected. Or perhaps *meant* to be seen.

It referenced the Ashford parcel indirectly, buried inside language about scheduling conflicts and interdepartmental coordination.

No accusations.
No threats.
Just delay.

Carolyn read it once, then set it aside.

"They're slowing themselves down," Mason said.

"That costs them," she replied.

"For now," he said.

Carolyn stepped out into the evening, boots settling into dirt that had never asked permission to exist.

She walked the fence line—not to inspect it, but to inhabit it. To remind herself that holding wasn't symbolic. It was physical. Repetitive. Often boring.

At the gate, she stopped.

The hinge creaked softly when she touched it.

She didn't open it.

She didn't need to.

Behind her, the house lights glowed steady. Ahead, the land rolled on, unchanged by documents, unmoved by deadlines.

Somewhere else—an office, a meeting room, a hallway—someone was deciding what to do with a problem that wouldn't resolve itself on schedule.

Carolyn turned back toward the house.

She hadn't won anything.

But she hadn't conceded either.

And in Wyoming, that was the difference between being managed and being remembered.

Chapter 9

REASONABLE ASSUMPTIONS

The site visit was scheduled without consultation.

That was the miscalculation.

The email arrived mid-morning, buried beneath neutral subject lines and copied to just enough people to look procedural.

Multi-Agency Site Review — Confirmed
Pursuant to ongoing compliance review, representatives from Land & Access, Environmental Standards, and County Survey will conduct a preliminary site assessment of trust-held parcels for alignment verification.

No request.
No agenda.
No acknowledgment of prior refusal.

Just a date.
And a time.

Carolyn read it once, then forwarded it to Mason without comment.

He called within a minute.

"They didn't ask," he said.

"No," she replied.

"They're treating silence as assent."

"Yes."

"That's new," Mason said.

"It is," Carolyn agreed. "Which means something changed."

The county office treated the confirmation as a formality.

Raina Harlan stood at the copier watching pages stack, listening to a junior staffer explain logistics like weather.

"Survey will want access to the south line," the woman said. "Environmental's mostly observational. Sheriff's Office is listed as standby."

"Standby for what?" Raina asked.

The staffer hesitated.

"Presence," she said.

Raina nodded, expression unreadable.

Presence was not neutral.
It was anticipatory.

"Has the trust responded?" Raina asked.

"No," the staffer said. "But the window elapsed."

Raina took the printed packet and flipped through it.

"Elapsed," she repeated. "Or ignored?"

The staffer flushed.

"They didn't object," she said.

Raina closed the packet.

"They didn't consent," she said.

That distinction mattered. Raina knew it.

She also knew what her calendar now implied.

Kade arrived the evening before the scheduled visit.

Not because he'd been asked.

Because sequence had shifted.

He didn't bring anything with him. No files. No opinions. Just the habit of standing where lines mattered.

"They're coming tomorrow," Carolyn said.

"I know," Kade replied.

Mason watched him carefully.

"They didn't ask," Mason said.

Kade nodded.

"That's the assumption," he said. "They think the quiet worked."

"And?" Carolyn asked.

"And it did," Kade said. "On paper."

He walked to the window and looked out at the drive, tracing the arc vehicles always followed without realizing they were repeating someone else's idea of access.

"They're counting on frictionless compliance," he continued. "No confrontation. No refusal. Just presence becoming precedent."

Mason crossed his arms.

"So what happens if we don't stop them?" he asked.

Kade turned.

"They stop themselves," he said.

Carolyn waited.

"If they arrive without consent," Kade continued, "they're no longer reviewing. They're acting."

"And that matters," Mason said.

"It matters because it forces a record," Kade replied. "And records are the only thing institutions fear."

Silence followed.

Carolyn looked at the email again.

"They'll show up anyway," she said.

"Yes," Kade replied.

"And if I block them?" she asked.

"They escalate," he said. "Badge steps forward. Tone shifts. Everyone loses altitude."

Mason frowned.

"And if she doesn't?" he asked.

Kade's answer was immediate.

"Then the mistake is theirs," he said.

The morning arrived clear and cold.

Three vehicles turned onto the drive exactly on time.

White.
White.
Gray.

They stopped short of the gate.

People stepped out with clipboards and vests, moving with the choreography of those who believed the door would open if they waited long enough.

Carolyn stood on the porch.

She didn't wave.

She didn't approach.

She didn't retreat.

Raina Harlan exited the second vehicle and paused when she saw her.

Not surprised.
Just alert.

She walked forward alone.

"Ms. Ashford," she called. "Good morning."

"Good morning," Carolyn replied.

Raina gestured lightly behind her.

"We're here for the preliminary assessment," she said. "Observational only."

Carolyn didn't move.

"I didn't consent," she said.

Raina nodded.

"We notified you," she replied.

"You scheduled yourselves," Carolyn said.

Raina considered her.

"That's how these things usually proceed," she said.

Carolyn held her gaze.

"Usually," she replied, "assumes agreement."

A beat passed.

Behind Raina, survey staff shifted. One checked his watch.

Raina lowered her voice.

"We're not here to challenge your position," she said. "We're here to document."

Carolyn's voice stayed level.

"You can document from the road," she said.

Raina exhaled.

"Ms. Ashford," she said quietly, "refusal creates complications."

Carolyn nodded.

"Assumptions already did," she said.

Raina glanced past her—toward the house, the land, the people who would eventually pay for the county's confidence.

Then she made her mistake.

"Given the ongoing review," she said, "your cooperation would reflect favorably."

The word hung between them.

Favorably.

Carolyn didn't react outwardly.

Inside, something clicked.

"Favor with whom?" she asked.

Raina didn't answer immediately.

She couldn't.

And that was enough.

Carolyn stepped aside—just far enough to clear the porch.

"You can stay right there," she said. "You cannot enter."

The group waited.

The wind moved through the grass.

No one advanced.

No one retreated.

Kade stood back, hands in his pockets, watching the line hold without intervention.

Finally, Raina nodded once.

"We'll reschedule," she said.

"Please don't," Carolyn replied. "Ask instead."

Raina met her eyes.

That wasn't how this was supposed to go.

By afternoon, the emails began.

Not angry.
Not accusatory.
Concerned.

The phrase *"miscommunication"* appeared three times.

Mason read one aloud.

"They think this was a misunderstanding," he said.

Carolyn closed the laptop.

"It wasn't," she said.

Kade nodded.

"They assumed quiet meant compliance," he said. "That's the first real error."

"And now?" Mason asked.

Kade looked at the land.

"Now they have to decide whether to escalate *openly*," he said, "or retreat *awkwardly*."

Carolyn stood.

"And either choice costs them," she said.

"Yes," Kade replied. "Which is why they'll try something else."

She looked at him.

"Next vector?" she asked.

Kade didn't answer right away.

He watched the road empty.

"Legitimacy," he said finally. "They'll try to move it."

Chapter 10

STANDING QUESTIONS

The letter came from an office Carolyn hadn't dealt with before.

That was the point.

Not Land & Access.
Not Environmental Standards.
Not the Sheriff's Office.

County Administrative Review Board

The language was careful. Polite. Almost deferential.

As part of an ongoing evaluation of trust-held parcels within the county, the Board is conducting a routine clarification of governance structures to ensure transparency, continuity, and appropriate representation.

Clarification.

Governance.

Representation.

Carolyn read it twice, then once more without focusing on the words—only the shape of the ask.

This wasn't about access.

It was about **authority**.

Mason arrived with coffee she didn't ask for and a look that said he'd already seen this kind of move somewhere else.

"They've changed rooms," he said.

"Yes," Carolyn replied. "And chairs."

He sat across from her at the table, the letter between them.

"This board doesn't have teeth," he said.

"No," she agreed. "But they have minutes."

Mason nodded.

Minutes turned questions into record.

Records turned uncertainty into leverage.

"They want to know who speaks for the trust," Mason said.

Carolyn didn't answer immediately.

She stared at the letter.

"They want to know if *I* do," she said.

The meeting room at the county building was smaller than she expected.

No seal on the wall. No flags. Just a table, a clock, and a woman with a yellow legal pad who introduced herself as *recording secretary* and nothing else.

Three board members sat already.

None of them stood.

None of them smiled.

Carolyn took the offered seat and placed her folder on the table—closed.

She waited.

The chair cleared his throat.

"Ms. Ashford," he said. "Thank you for coming."

"You asked," she replied.

A pause.

"Yes," he said. "We appreciate your cooperation."

Carolyn didn't correct him.

"That word was doing too much work today."

The questions began gently.

"How long has the trust been active?"
"Who drafted the original charter?"
"Is decision-making centralized or distributed?"

Carolyn answered cleanly. Precisely. Without elaboration.

The recording secretary's pen moved steadily.

Then the shape shifted.

"One concern raised," the chair said, glancing down at his notes, "is continuity."

"Continuity of what?" Carolyn asked.

"Of representation," he replied. "If, for example, a trustee were unavailable."

Unavailable.

Not *removed*.
Not *challenged*.

Just... gone.

"The trust has provisions," Carolyn said. "They're documented."

"Yes," the chair agreed. "But provisions don't always reflect practical realities."

Carolyn met his eyes.

"They reflect legal ones," she said.

Another pause.

A woman on the board leaned forward slightly.

"Ms. Ashford," she said, "this isn't adversarial. We're simply ensuring that decisions affecting multiple stakeholders are made transparently."

"Which stakeholders?" Carolyn asked.

The woman hesitated.

"Adjacent landholders," she said. "The county. Future development interests."

Carolyn nodded.

"None of whom are beneficiaries," she said.

"No," the woman agreed. "But they are impacted."

There it was.

Impact was the new word.

Kade waited outside the building, leaning against the truck like he'd been there long enough not to be noticed.

When Carolyn stepped out, he straightened without rushing.

"They didn't ask about land," he said.

"No," she replied. "They asked about me."

He nodded.

"They're testing standing," he said.

"They're suggesting it's… conditional."

"Yes," Kade said. "That's the move."

Mason joined them, jacket already on like he wanted distance from the room they'd just left.

"They want someone easier to talk to," he said.

Kade didn't smile.

"They want someone who answers questions the way they expect," he said.

Carolyn looked back at the building.

"They didn't accuse," she said.

"They never do," Kade replied. "Accusations create resistance. Questions create doubt."

Later that evening, Carolyn sat alone at the table, the board's letter beside her, her notes from the meeting stacked neatly on top.

She replayed the questions—not what they'd asked, but what they'd *implied*.

What if you're not the right one?
What if this is bigger than you?
What if legitimacy requires permission?

She closed her eyes.

She didn't feel angry.

She felt measured.

Which was worse.

Her phone buzzed.

A text from a number she hadn't saved but recognized immediately.

Friend:
So who is this Kade? You've mentioned him three times now.

Carolyn stared at the screen longer than necessary.

She typed, deleted, typed again.

Carolyn:
He's local. He understands the terrain.

A moment passed.

Friend:
That's still not an answer.

Carolyn exhaled.

Carolyn:
He's disciplined. Careful. Doesn't say much.

Three dots appeared. Disappeared. Appeared again.

Friend:
And that makes you feel...?

Carolyn set the phone face-down on the table.

She didn't answer.

Not because she didn't know.

Because knowing felt like another kind of vulnerability.

Outside, the land held the quiet the way it always had—without comment, without permission.

Inside the county building, a new file tab had been created.

Standing: Clarification Pending

And for the first time since the trust was formed, the question wasn't whether the land could be held.

It was whether the one holding it would be allowed to remain.

Chapter 11

THE INVITATION

The invitation arrived by mail and email.

That alone told Carolyn what it was.

County notices came one way.
Social obligations came another.

This one came embossed on heavy stock, cream-colored, the kind of paper that suggested permanence and good lighting.

The Northern Wyoming Development Forum
An evening discussion on regional continuity, infrastructure alignment, and responsible stewardship.

Responsible stewardship.

Carolyn read it twice.

The date fell neatly between the administrative review and the next compliance window.

Of course it did.

Mason looked at the card and snorted softly.

"That's not a meeting," he said. "That's a room."

"Yes," Carolyn replied. "And rooms decide things before votes ever do."

Kade stood by the window, watching a pickup idle at the edge of the road before turning away again.

"They're inviting you to be reasonable," he said.

"And if I decline?" Carolyn asked.

"They'll say you're difficult," Mason replied. "Not hostile. Just... inflexible."

Carolyn nodded.

"And if I go?" she asked.

Kade answered this time.

"Then you'll be observed," he said. "Not for what you say. For what you *don't*."

The venue was a restored lodge just outside town—stone fireplace, long beams, the faint smell of money that liked to think of itself as local.

Carolyn arrived alone.

Not because she had to.

Because arriving with anyone would have shifted the frame.

The room was already full. Not crowded—curated.

People turned when she entered. Not heads snapping. Just attention adjusting.

She felt it immediately.

This wasn't a welcome.

It was a **measurement**.

She moved toward the bar, ordered a water, and stood where she could see the room without being centered in it.

Conversations continued.

Then changed.

She heard her name once. Twice.

Never spoken directly to her.

A man approached—mid-forties, clean boots, practiced smile.

"Ms. Ashford," he said. "Glad you could make it."

"Thank you for the invitation," she replied.

He gestured vaguely around the room.

"This is really about alignment," he said. "Finding common ground."

"Between whom?" she asked.

He smiled again.

"Stakeholders," he said.

She nodded.

"That word travels," she said.

The smile tightened. Just a little.

She felt Kade before she saw him.

Not because she expected him.

Because the air around her settled.

He didn't come to her immediately. He took a position near the wall, drink untouched, listening more than participating.

That was the mistake they hadn't anticipated.

They'd assumed she would arrive alone.

They hadn't counted on **familiar gravity**.

A woman joined Carolyn at the bar.

"Carolyn," she said, offering her hand. "Linda Harper. Regional planning."

Carolyn shook it.

"Interesting week to host this," Carolyn said.

Linda laughed lightly.

"It's always an interesting week," she said. "But tonight's about relationships."

Carolyn met her eyes.

"Relationships are clearer when expectations are stated," she said.

Linda nodded.

"Exactly," she said. "And expectations are easier to meet when communication is open."

Carolyn took a sip of water.

"Then this should be productive," she said.

Across the room, Kade watched the choreography.

Who approached.
Who avoided.
Who spoke near Carolyn without addressing her.

He moved once—just enough to change sightlines.

That's when it happened.

A man—older, confident—stepped into Carolyn's space without asking.

"You're holding up progress," he said quietly. Not accusatory. Almost sympathetic.

Carolyn turned to face him.

"Progress toward what?" she asked.

He smiled.

"Toward inevitability," he said.

She held his gaze.

"Inevitable things don't need help," she said.

The smile faltered.

Kade didn't intervene.

He didn't need to.

The man stepped back on his own.

Later, as people filtered toward the fireplace and speeches that weren't speeches began, Carolyn found herself beside Kade without planning it.

"You didn't say anything," she said quietly.

"That was the point," he replied.

She nodded.

"They wanted me to speak," she said.

"Yes," he agreed.

"So they could place me," she added.

"Yes."

Silence passed between them—not awkward. Just full.

"You shouldn't stay long," he said.

"I know," she replied.

A pause.

Then, without thinking—

"Carrie," he said, low. "They're circling. You don't owe them patience."

She froze.

Just for a beat.

"No one ever called me *Carrie*," she said quietly. "Except my dad."

The space between them shifted—subtly, irreversibly.

Kade straightened immediately.

"I'm sorry," he said. "That wasn't—"

"It's fine," she said, too quickly. Then softer: "I haven't heard it in a long time."

He nodded once.

"I won't say it again," he said.

She believed him.

She left ten minutes later.

No goodbye tour. No explanations.

Just absence.

In the room she left behind, conclusions were drawn that no one would write down.

Outside, the night was cold and clean.

"You okay?" Kade asked, already turning toward his truck.

"Yes," she said. Then, after a beat: "Thank you."

"For what?" he asked.

"For not trying to help," she replied.

He smiled faintly.

"Anytime," he said.

He left first.

Which was exactly right.

Chapter 12

PATTERN

By the time the third notice arrived, Carolyn stopped reading them individually.

Not because they weren't important—but because they were no longer discrete.

They had begun to rhyme.

Different letterheads.
Different departments.
Different language.

Same cadence.

Requests for clarification.
Reminders of compliance windows.
Notes referencing prior correspondence "for continuity."

None of it accusatory.
None of it urgent.

Together, it formed something else entirely.

A tempo.

Carolyn laid the documents side by side on the table, not sorting them by date, but by tone. Once she did, the order became obvious.

"They're not escalating," Mason said over speakerphone. "They're standardizing."

"Yes," Carolyn replied. "They're teaching a rhythm."

Kade stood nearby, hands loose at his sides, watching without interrupting.

"Rhythms condition," he said.

Carolyn nodded.

"That's the point," she said. "They want compliance to feel automatic."

She drafted no response that afternoon.

That, too, was deliberate.

Responding too early would have placed her inside the rhythm. Responding too late would have allowed urgency to define the exchange.

Instead, she waited until the pattern revealed itself fully.

By evening, it had.

Three agencies.
Five communications.
Zero demands.

Just presence.

The next morning, Mason arrived in person.

"They're careful," he said, reviewing the spread. "Someone upstream is coordinating this."

"Yes," Carolyn said. "But not owning it."

"That's unusual," he replied.

"No," she corrected. "It's transitional."

She slid one email forward.

"They're still seeing if I'll move on my own," she said. "If I do, no one has to sign anything."

Kade looked at the page once, then away.

"I've seen what happens when people explain themselves too early," he said.

Carolyn didn't ask where.

She didn't need to.

By midday, the pressure shifted—not louder, but closer.

A follow-up email arrived referencing her silence.

Polite.
Measured.

We just want to make sure we're aligned.

Aligned.

Carolyn smiled faintly.

Alignment was what institutions called agreement before it was earned.

She typed a single sentence in reply:

Please advise if there is a specific statutory requirement requiring action at this time.

No greeting.
No justification.

Just a question.

The response took six hours.

When it came, it was shorter than the request.

We'll review and revert.

Carolyn closed the laptop.

"They've lost the rhythm," Mason said.

"No," she replied. "They've revealed it."

Kade watched the light fade through the window.

"It wasn't escalation," he said.

Carolyn finished the thought.

"It was conditioning."

Outside, the wind moved through the grass the way it always had.

Unconcerned.
Patient.

The land didn't respond to rhythm.

Only to force—or time.

And time, for the moment, was hers.

Chapter 13

CONDITIONING

The pressure returned the same way it always did.

Not louder.

More frequent.

The email arrived at 8:17 a.m.

Then another at 9:02.

Different senders.
Different departments.
Same shape.

Clarification requested.
Timeline adjustment proposed.
Follow-up pending.

Carolyn didn't answer either.

By noon, Mason had counted seven points of contact.

"None of these matter on their own," he said. "That's what makes them dangerous."

"Yes," Carolyn replied. "They're training response."

Kade stood near the doorway, listening to cadence rather than content.

"They want to see if the third or fourth nudge gets a reaction," he said. "That's conditioning."

"Like animals," Mason said.

"Like institutions," Kade corrected. "They repeat until behavior changes."

Carolyn looked up.

"And if behavior doesn't change?"

Kade met her eyes.

"Then they escalate form," he said. "Not force. Form."

The next move arrived disguised as help.

A call from County Mediation Services—an office that hadn't existed until recently, staffed by people who spoke softly and used words like *facilitation* and *de-escalation*.

The woman on the line sounded earnest.

"We're here to prevent misunderstandings," she said. "Sometimes direct channels become strained."

Carolyn smiled faintly.

"Strained how?" she asked.

"Well," the woman replied carefully, "there seems to be some hesitation on both sides."

Carolyn waited.

"Your hesitance to engage," the woman clarified. "And the county's concern about progress."

"Progress toward what?" Carolyn asked.

A pause.

"Alignment," the woman said.

Carolyn ended the call without raising her voice.

"They're offering me a cushion," she said afterward. "So they can say I refused it."

"Yes," Mason said.

"And cushions absorb impact," Kade added. "They want to make the next step look unreasonable."

By midweek, the perimeter tightened again.

A delivery truck missed its window.
A survey map came back "incomplete."
A routine utility check required additional documentation.

None of it illegal.
All of it exhausting.

Carolyn felt the rhythm now.

Pressure.
Pause.
Repeat.

The goal wasn't to break her.

It was to **normalize adjustment**.

That night, she lay awake longer than she admitted.

Not thinking about the county.

Thinking about sequence.

She replayed meetings, emails, expressions—where she might have bent without noticing.

Her phone buzzed once.

Friend:
Still holding the line?

Carolyn stared at the message.

Carolyn:
Yes.

A beat.

Friend:
You don't usually answer that fast.

Carolyn set the phone face-down.

She wasn't ready to talk.

Talking turned recognition into narrative.

Narrative turned strength into explanation.

She needed neither.

The trust meeting the following morning was quiet in the way rooms get when people arrive early and choose seats carefully.

The secondary trustee—the one who'd suggested a liaison—sat closer to the door than usual.

He spoke gently.

"I'm not questioning leadership," he said. "Just wondering whether there's a way to reduce exposure."

"Exposure to what?" Carolyn asked.

"To… scrutiny," he replied.

Carolyn nodded.

"Scrutiny follows authority," she said. "Deflection invites more."

The room held its breath.

Kade watched without intervening.

Mason took notes.

No one argued.

No one agreed.

That was new.

Afterward, as people filtered out, Mason leaned toward her.

"They're not with you," he said quietly. "But they're not against you either."

Carolyn stood.

"That's the point of conditioning," she said. "To create neutrality."

Outside, the wind had shifted direction.

Carolyn walked the edge of the property alone, boots tracing the boundary line she knew by heart now.

This was what they wanted her to feel.

Fatigue without injury.
Doubt without accusation.
Visibility without control.

Behind her, a vehicle approached and stopped at a respectful distance.

Kade stepped out but didn't come closer.

He waited until she turned.

"They're repeating," she said.

"Yes," he replied.

"To see if I change," she added.

"Yes."

She crossed her arms—not cold, just bracing.

"And if I don't?"

Kade didn't answer right away.

"They'll escalate the cost," he said finally. "Not to punish you. To teach others."

Carolyn nodded.

She understood now.

Conditioning wasn't about her.

It was about everyone watching her.

She looked back at the land.

"Then I stay consistent," she said.

Kade's voice was steady.

"That's how you break conditioning," he said. "You refuse to vary."

She exhaled slowly.

The wind moved through the grass again—same direction, same sound.

Not resistance.

Persistence.

Chapter 14

VARIANCE

The call came from a familiar number.

That was intentional.

Raina Harlan didn't speak like someone escalating.

She spoke like someone offering a solution.

"Ms. Ashford," she said, voice measured. "I wanted to follow up. There may be a way to reduce the friction we've been seeing."

Carolyn didn't respond immediately.

She let silence do its work.

"I'm listening," she said finally.

"There's a variance request pending," Raina continued. "A narrow one. Limited scope. It would allow certain activity to proceed while broader questions are clarified."

"Which activity?" Carolyn asked.

"Utility access," Raina said. "Temporary. Observational oversight only."

Carolyn closed her eyes briefly.

Variance.

The word was calibrated to sound reasonable.

A pause, a bridge, a gesture.

"What's the cost?" Carolyn asked.

Raina hesitated.

"Cooperation," she said. "Transparency."

Carolyn smiled faintly.

"Those words are doing a lot of work today," she replied.

Mason read the summary twice.

"They're offering relief," he said. "Which means they want something in return."

"They want deviation," Kade said from the doorway. "One exception."

Carolyn nodded.

"And exceptions become reference points," she said.

"Yes," Kade agreed. "Conditioning escalates to variance when repetition fails."

Mason frowned.

"So if we refuse, they claim we're unreasonable," he said. "If we accept, they claim precedent."

Carolyn leaned back in her chair.

"They're not asking me to surrender authority," she said. "They're asking me to demonstrate flexibility."

"And flexibility," Mason said, "is observable."

Carolyn looked at Kade.

"They want me to bend where it looks harmless," she said.

Kade met her gaze.

"Because harmless bends are the easiest to repeat," he said.

That afternoon, the paperwork arrived.

Clean.
Limited.
Full of language that softened impact without changing effect.

Temporary.
Non-binding.
Subject to review.

Every clause ended with *as determined by the county.*

Carolyn traced one paragraph with her finger.

"They're asking me to sign something that doesn't change anything," she said.

Mason shook his head.

"It changes everything," he replied. "It proves you'll adjust under pressure."

Silence followed.

This was the hardest kind of decision.

Not refusal.

Acceptance with consequence.

Carolyn stood and walked to the window, staring out at the land that hadn't moved despite everything done in its name.

"This is how people lose ground," she said quietly. "Not by force. By accommodation."

Kade spoke carefully.

"They don't need you to lose," he said. "They need you to *vary*."

She nodded.

"And if I don't?" she asked.

"They escalate again," Kade replied. "Different vector."

Carolyn exhaled slowly.

That evening, the trust gathered.

Not formally. Not urgently.

Just enough people in the room to feel the weight of choice.

Carolyn laid the variance request on the table.

"This is what they're offering," she said. "Temporary relief."

A murmur moved through the room.

The secondary trustee spoke first.

"This could buy us time," he said. "Let things cool."

"Or signal weakness," another replied.

Carolyn listened without interruption.

When the room quieted, she spoke.

"Variance isn't compromise," she said. "It's calibration."

She looked at each of them in turn.

"If I sign this, I teach them that pressure works. Not today—but eventually."

Silence followed.

No one argued.

No one volunteered support.

That, too, was information.

Later, when the room had emptied and the lights were lower, Carolyn sat alone at the table, the unsigned variance before her.

Her phone buzzed.

Friend:
Still in Wyoming?

Carolyn hesitated.

Carolyn:
Yes.

A moment.

Friend:
You sound tired even in text.

Carolyn looked up as footsteps approached.

Kade stopped a few feet away.

"Decision night," he said.

"Yes," she replied.

He didn't look at the paper.

"Whatever you decide," he said, "make sure it's repeatable."

She considered that.

Not whether it was defensible.

Whether she could live with it happening again.

She slid the variance back into the folder.

"I won't sign," she said.

Kade nodded once.

"They'll notice," he said.

"Yes," she replied.

"And?" he asked.

Carolyn stood.

"And that's the point."

The refusal went out the next morning.

No speech.
No explanation.
Just a clean, professional decline.

By afternoon, the variance was gone.

By evening, the pressure returned—different shape, same intent.

The system had learned something.

So had she.

Chapter 15

THE QUIET PENALTY

The penalty didn't announce itself.

It arrived sideways, the way consequences always did when no one wanted to be seen delivering them.

Carolyn learned about it from the bank.

The call came mid-morning, polite and apologetic.

"We're reviewing the trust's account activity," the officer said. "Nothing alarming. Just... enhanced diligence."

"Triggered by what?" Carolyn asked.

A pause.

"County notation," the man replied. "Procedural."

Procedural was the word people used when they didn't want to say *pressure*.

Mason arrived an hour later with printouts he hadn't bothered to staple.

"They didn't freeze anything," he said. "They slowed it."

Carolyn read through the pages.

Payment verification delays.
Secondary approvals.
Requests for additional documentation already provided.

"They're touching liquidity," she said.

"Yes," Mason replied. "Just enough to be felt. Not enough to contest."

Carolyn leaned back.

"This isn't about money," she said.

"No," Mason agreed. "It's about comfort."

By afternoon, the effect spread.

A vendor asked for partial payment up front.
Another postponed work "pending clarity."
A third quietly stepped away altogether.

No explanations.

Just distance.

Kade watched it happen without comment.

When he spoke, it was only to name shape.

"They're teaching people to associate you with friction," he said. "Not danger. Delay."

Carolyn nodded.

"They want me expensive," she said again.

"Yes," Kade replied. "But only to others."

That evening, Carolyn sat alone at the table longer than usual.

Not working.

Accounting.

Not numbers.

Cost.

Every delay, every pause, every second look now carried her name.

Not publicly.

Socially.

The quiet penalty was working exactly as designed.

Her phone buzzed.

Friend:
You disappeared today.

Carolyn stared at the screen.

Carolyn:
Long day.

Friend:
You don't say that anymore. You used to say "productive."

Carolyn exhaled slowly.

She didn't reply.

She didn't want to explain fatigue.

Explanation invited suggestion.

Suggestion invited doubt.

The trust meeting that followed was shorter than the last.

People spoke carefully now.

Questions carried more qualifiers.

"What if…"
"Have we considered…"
"Just to be safe…"

Carolyn listened.

She didn't interrupt.

When it ended, Mason leaned close.

"They're not asking you to step down," he said. "They're asking you to absorb."

"Yes," Carolyn replied.

"And?" he asked.

She stood.

"And absorption has limits."

Later, outside, the sky pressed low and gray.

Carolyn walked the perimeter again, slower this time.

Not because she was tired.

Because she was measuring.

Kade waited near the fence, hands in his pockets, giving her space.

"They're not escalating publicly," she said.

"No," he replied. "They're waiting."

"For what?" she asked.

"For you to change something small," he said. "Anything."

She stopped.

"And if I don't?"

Kade's answer came without emphasis.

"They increase the penalty," he said. "Or they change the target."

Carolyn turned to face him.

"To whom?"

Kade met her eyes.

"To someone who matters to you."

The weight of that landed differently.

Not fear.

Focus.

She folded her arms—not defensively, but decisively.

"Then we plan for that," she said.

Kade nodded.

"That's the correct response."

That night, sleep came late.

Not because of anxiety.

Because of vigilance.

Her mind kept inventory—not of threats, but of dependencies.

Who relied on the trust.
Who relied on her.
Who could be made uncomfortable without explanation.

In the dark, a single thought surfaced—not analyzed, not lingered on.

Holding costs more when you're visible.

She didn't push it away.

She filed it.

By morning, the system had moved again.

A new memo circulated.

Neutral. Administrative. Unremarkable.

But this time, it wasn't addressed to her.

It was addressed **around** her.

And that was the quietest penalty of all.

Chapter 16

THE OTHER OPTION

The proposal didn't come to Carolyn.

That was the design.

It surfaced through a third channel—quiet, professional, almost courteous.

Mason learned about it from a colleague who shouldn't have known anything.

"They're floating an alternative," he said when he arrived. "Off the record."

Carolyn didn't look up.

"Alternative to what?" she asked.

"To you," Mason replied.

That got her attention.

The outline was simple. Elegant. Almost generous.

A regional stewardship council.
Temporary oversight authority.
Local representation "for continuity."

Someone who understood the county.
Someone "easier to coordinate with."
Someone who would absorb pressure *instead of reflecting it.*

"They're not saying you're a problem," Mason said. "They're saying the structure is."

Carolyn nodded.

"They're saying I'm inconvenient," she said.

"Yes," Mason replied. "And inconvenience is solvable."

Kade listened without interruption.

When Mason finished, Kade spoke once.

"They're offering an exit that preserves everyone's dignity," he said.

Carolyn looked at him.

"Whose?" she asked.

Kade didn't hesitate.

"Theirs," he said.

The language, once she saw it, was unmistakable.

Not hostile.
Not accusatory.
Just… accommodating.

This would reduce burden.
This would streamline coordination.
This would allow you to focus on higher priorities.

Higher priorities.

As if holding the line were a distraction.

"They're trying to move me sideways," Carolyn said. "Out of frame."

"Yes," Kade replied. "Without asking you to leave."

Mason leaned forward.

"They'll pitch it as relief," he said. "They'll say it protects you."

Carolyn closed the folder.

"Protection that costs authority," she said.

That evening, the trust gathered again.

This time, the room felt different.

Less tentative.

More practical.

The secondary trustee spoke carefully.

"This could take pressure off," he said. "We wouldn't be conceding anything. Just… redistributing responsibility."

Carolyn waited.

Another added, "It might be temporary."

Temporary again.

The word had been busy lately.

Carolyn stood.

"They are offering you comfort," she said. "At my expense."

Silence followed.

She didn't soften it.

"This is not about workload," she continued. "It's about who decides. And whether visibility is optional."

The secondary trustee shifted.

"No one's questioning your commitment," he said.

Carolyn met his eyes.

"They're questioning my utility," she replied.

After the meeting, the property was quiet in the way places get when decisions are circling but not landing.

Carolyn stepped outside.

The night was clear. Sharp.

Kade joined her after a moment, stopping a respectful distance away.

"They want you gone without saying gone," he said.

"Yes," she replied.

"And?" he asked.

She took a breath.

"And they think you'll let me," she said.

Kade frowned slightly.

"They think the trust will," he said.

Carolyn shook her head.

"They think *I* will," she said. "Because it's easier."

Kade didn't argue.

"Are you considering it?" he asked.

She looked at him.

"No," she said. "I'm measuring it."

He nodded.

"That's different," he said.

Later, alone, Carolyn sat with the proposal spread out in front of her.

It was persuasive.

That was the danger.

It offered:

- rest
- distance
- insulation
- plausibility

It asked for nothing overt.

Just absence.

Her phone buzzed.

Friend:
So… Wyoming still kicking your ass?

Carolyn almost smiled.

Carolyn:
It's trying to.

A moment passed.

Friend:
And this Kade guy—does he help?

Carolyn stared at the question.

She thought of steadiness.
Of silence.
Of a line that didn't move.

Carolyn:
He keeps me oriented.

Three dots appeared.

Then disappeared.

The friend didn't push.

By morning, the "other option" had momentum.

Emails circulated.

Meetings were suggested.

Names were floated.

All of them plausible.

All of them local.

All of them acceptable.

None of them her.

Carolyn stood at the window as the land caught first light.

This was the cleanest removal she'd ever seen.

No confrontation.

No victory.

Just replacement.

Behind her, footsteps approached.

Kade stopped.

"They're giving you a way out," he said.

Carolyn didn't turn.

"They're giving me a way to disappear," she replied.

Silence stretched.

Then she spoke—quiet, certain.

"I'm not done."

Kade nodded once.

"Then neither are they," he said.

Chapter 17

THE LINE MOVES

The notice went out without her name on it.

That was the tell.

It wasn't addressed to the trust.
It wasn't copied to her.
It didn't ask for acknowledgment.

It simply appeared—in inboxes that mattered.

Pursuant to revised coordination protocols, field activities adjacent to trust-held parcels will proceed under interim stewardship guidance until governance clarification is complete.

Interim stewardship.

Guidance.

Clarification.

Carolyn read the forwarded copy once, then set it down.

"They're behaving as if I've already stepped aside," she said.

Mason nodded grimly.

"They've created a parallel authority," he said. "Soft. Unofficial. Operational."

Kade stood near the doorway, hands still, listening.

"They didn't remove you," he said. "They stepped around you."

The first sign wasn't dramatic.

It was practical.

A utility truck turned where it hadn't before.

Not onto the land—close enough to signal intent.

Carolyn watched from the porch as it idled, a man inside consulting a tablet like the boundary had moved without anyone bothering to tell the ground.

She walked down the steps.

The truck didn't move.

She stopped ten feet short.

"You're not cleared," she said.

The driver hesitated.

"We've got interim authorization," he replied, holding up the screen. "County coordination."

Carolyn didn't raise her voice.

"You don't," she said. "You have an assumption."

The driver frowned.

"They said—"

"They're not here," Carolyn said. "I am."

Silence stretched.

Behind her, Kade remained still.

The driver made a decision.

He put the truck in reverse and backed out slowly, like someone leaving a room they hadn't meant to enter.

By noon, two more attempts followed.

Different vehicles.
Same posture.

No confrontation.

Just quiet testing.

"They're moving the line by repetition," Mason said. "Seeing if access becomes normalized."

"Yes," Carolyn replied. "Like conditioning."

Kade nodded.

"Except this time," he said, "they're not asking permission. They're acting as if it already exists."

"And if I respond every time?" Carolyn asked.

"They'll say you're obstructive," Mason said.

"And if I don't?" she asked.

"They'll say you consented," Kade replied.

That was the trap.

Action framed as aggression.
Silence framed as approval.

The county meeting request came mid-afternoon.

Not urgent.
Not mandatory.

To align expectations moving forward.

Carolyn declined without comment.

Minutes later, a follow-up arrived—more insistent in tone, still polite.

She declined again.

"They're recording refusal now," Mason said.

"Yes," Carolyn replied. "Let them."

That evening, the trust fractured—just slightly.

One trustee called privately.

"I heard they're moving ahead," he said. "Is that true?"

"They're trying," Carolyn replied.

"And if they succeed?" he asked.

"They won't," she said.

A pause.

"That sounds expensive," he said.

"Yes," Carolyn replied. "Holding always is."

He didn't argue.

But he didn't commit either.

Night fell clean and cold.

Carolyn walked the boundary again, boots steady, the line unchanged despite the day's attempts to redraw it.

Kade joined her at a distance.

"They're forcing a moment," he said.

"Yes," she replied.

"They want you to react publicly," he continued. "Or stop reacting at all."

She stopped walking.

"And if I do neither?" she asked.

Kade considered that.

"Then they have to decide whether authority exists without their permission," he said.

Carolyn looked out at the dark land.

"That's the question they don't like," she said.

Late that night, an email circulated internally—she saw it because someone forwarded it quietly.

Subject: Field Interference
Issue: Repeated on-site obstruction by trust representative.

Obstruction.

The word was doing its work now.

Carolyn read it without expression.

"They're reframing holding as interference," Mason said.

"Yes," she replied. "That was inevitable."

Kade spoke softly.

"They've moved the line," he said. "Now they're waiting to see if it holds."

Carolyn closed the laptop.

"It does," she said.

In the dark, alone, the weight finally registered—not emotionally, but physically.

Her shoulders ached.

Not from fear.

From constancy.

She stood still, letting the fatigue pass without permission to settle.

A thought surfaced—uninvited, brief, and unexamined.

Some lines require witnesses.

She didn't pursue it.

She didn't name it.

She simply stood.

By morning, the system would either retreat or escalate.

But the line had already been drawn.

Not on a map.

In behavior.

And for the first time, everyone involved understood the cost of pretending it had moved.

Chapter 18

WITNESSES

The first witness wasn't intentional.

It was a neighbor.

A ranch truck slowed on the county road, dust settling as the driver leaned out his window to watch Carolyn standing at the gate, arms relaxed at her sides, body angled—not blocking, just *there*.

The truck rolled on.

That was enough.

By midmorning, two more vehicles passed slower than usual.

One stopped outright.

No one approached.
No one filmed.

But eyes stayed longer than they needed to.

"Word's moving," Mason said later. "Not officially."

"Never officially," Carolyn replied.

Kade stood a few steps back, tracking sightlines instead of faces.

"Witnesses change cost calculations," he said. "For everyone."

The county vehicle arrived just before noon.

Unmarked.
Clean.
Confident.

It parked deliberately inside the line where people had learned not to stop.

A man stepped out—late thirties, jacket instead of vest, no clipboard visible.

This wasn't field work.

This was messaging.

Carolyn walked forward alone.

"You're inside the boundary," she said.

The man smiled faintly.

"We're observing," he replied.

"From here?" she asked.

"Yes," he said. "Briefly."

Carolyn didn't raise her voice.

"You're not authorized," she said.

The man glanced back at his car, then around—not at the land, but at the road.

At who might be watching.

"We're not interfering," he said. "We're documenting."

Carolyn nodded.

"You can document from the shoulder," she said. "Or you can leave."

The man hesitated.

Not because he was uncertain.

Because he was calculating.

Behind Carolyn, Kade shifted position—not closer, just enough to be visible.

A second vehicle slowed on the road and stopped.

A third followed.

Witnesses.

The man exhaled.

"This doesn't need to escalate," he said quietly.

Carolyn met his eyes.

"Then don't," she replied.

He held the look for a moment longer.

Then he got back in the car and backed out slowly.

No apology.

No acknowledgment.

But the message had failed.

That afternoon, the language changed again.

Emails circulated with new phrasing.

Situational complexity.
Community sensitivity.
Reputational considerations.

They were feeling the watchers.

"They don't like being seen applying pressure," Mason said.

"No," Carolyn replied. "They prefer inevitability."

Kade nodded.

"And inevitability doesn't photograph well," he said.

Later, alone for a moment, Carolyn stood on the porch, watching the land breathe under the weight of attention it hadn't asked for.

She felt it then—not fear, not doubt.

Responsibility.

Witnesses didn't just protect.

They demanded consistency.

If she varied now, it wouldn't just be noted.

It would be remembered.

Footsteps approached.

Kade stopped beside her—not touching, not intruding.

"They'll recalibrate," he said. "They always do."

"And if they don't?" she asked.

"Then they escalate openly," he replied. "Which changes the game."

She nodded.

Open escalation meant records.

Records meant scrutiny.

The system avoided that unless forced.

That evening, the call came from someone new.

A local business owner she hadn't met but knew by reputation.

"I saw what happened today," he said. "Just wanted you to know—you weren't alone out there."

"Thank you," Carolyn replied.

No promises were made.

None were needed.

After the call, she sat quietly, hands folded, absorbing what it meant to be seen not as a problem—but as a reference.

Her phone buzzed.

Friend:
Are people watching now?

Carolyn paused.

Carolyn:
Yes.

A beat.

Friend:
That's heavier than it sounds.

Carolyn looked out at the darkening land.

Carolyn:
Yes.

She didn't say more.

Night fell without incident.

No vehicles.
No emails.

Just quiet.

But it wasn't relief.

It was recalculation.

The system was deciding whether witnesses were a deterrent—or an obstacle to be removed.

Carolyn stood at the edge of the property one last time before going inside.

Behind her, Kade remained where he always did.

Present.

Unmoving.

A line doesn't hold because one person stands it.

It holds because others see it held—and decide what that means for them.

Tomorrow, the system would choose.

But tonight, the line had witnesses.

And that changed everything.

Chapter 19

ESCALATION THRESHOLD

The quiet didn't last.

It never did.

By mid-morning, Carolyn could feel it—not through calls or notices, but through absence. The kind that meant people were meeting without her.

She learned it from Mason first.

"They're in session," he said when he arrived. "County execs. Closed door."

"No agenda?" she asked.

"None published."

Carolyn nodded.

That meant the agenda was *decision*.

The next move came faster than the last.

A formal notice—finally.

Not dramatic.
Not punitive.

Just precise.

Notice of Coordinated Compliance Action
Effective immediately, county departments will conduct a synchronized review of trust-adjacent operations to ensure alignment with regional standards.

Synchronized.

That word mattered.

"They're aligning departments," Mason said. "No more staggered pressure."

"Yes," Carolyn replied. "They're consolidating authority."

Kade stood near the window, watching the road.

"That's the threshold," he said.

"Explain," Carolyn said.

"When systems stop testing and start coordinating," he replied, "they've decided the risk of visibility is worth it."

By noon, vehicles were staged at different points along the county road.

Not entering.

Not retreating.

Just present.

Different markings.
Different agencies.

One posture.

"They want a response," Mason said.

"They want me to flinch," Carolyn replied.

Kade nodded.

"They want a public reaction they can label," he said. "Anything that justifies form."

Carolyn stepped onto the porch again.

She didn't approach the vehicles.

She didn't retreat inside.

She stood where she'd stood before.

Holding.

The first official approached—not in uniform, but with credentials visible at his belt like reassurance.

"Ms. Ashford," he said. "We're here to coordinate access for routine compliance."

Carolyn met his gaze.

"You don't have consent," she said.

"We have jurisdiction," he replied.

"That's not the same thing," she said.

The man smiled thinly.

"It is when exercised," he said.

Witnesses gathered again.

Two ranch trucks.
A woman with a phone she didn't raise.
A man who leaned against his fence and waited.

The official noticed.

His smile faded.

Behind Carolyn, Kade shifted—not forward, not back.

Just enough to be visible.

The official took a breath.

"This doesn't need to become something," he said.

Carolyn's voice stayed level.

"Then don't make it one," she replied.

A pause.

The official glanced at the vehicles.

At the road.

At the watchers.

"This is coordinated," he said. "You can't stop all of us."

Carolyn nodded.

"I don't need to," she said. "You need me to move."

Silence stretched.

That was the standoff.

The radio crackled from one of the vehicles.

Low voices.
Brief.

The official stepped back half a pace.

"We'll proceed from the perimeter," he said.

Carolyn inclined her head.

"Thank you," she replied.

He didn't like that.

But he accepted it.

By late afternoon, the county issued a follow-up.

Measured. Defensive.

Given observed sensitivities, field activities will remain off-site pending further clarification.

They hadn't won.

They hadn't lost.

They had paused at the edge.

"They crossed the threshold," Mason said that evening. "And felt the cost."

"Yes," Carolyn replied. "Which means next time won't be tentative."

Kade nodded.

"They'll either formalize," he said. "Or they'll retreat."

"And which do you expect?" Mason asked.

Kade didn't answer immediately.

"They don't like retreat," he said finally. "It looks like weakness."

Carolyn looked out at the land, now quiet again.

"Then they'll choose daylight," she said.

"Yes," Kade replied. "And daylight leaves records."

That night, as she prepared to sleep, the weight returned—not heavy, but insistent.

Not fear.

Anticipation.

She understood now what they were asking of her.

Not compliance.

Endurance.

The escalation threshold had been reached.

Next time, the system wouldn't test.

It would declare.

And when it did, the line wouldn't just be held.

It would be named.

Chapter 20

DECLARATION

The declaration came at 9:03 a.m.

It didn't arrive by accident.
It didn't arrive quietly.

It arrived everywhere at once.

Email.
Posted notice.
Shared memo.

Same language. Same timing.

No room for reinterpretation.

Declaration of Coordinated Jurisdictional Authority

In the interest of regional continuity, public safety, and responsible stewardship, the county hereby asserts unified jurisdictional oversight over all trust-adjacent operations pending final governance clarification.

Asserted.

Oversight.

Pending.

They had crossed the line they'd avoided for weeks.

They had named themselves.

Carolyn read it once.

Then she stood.

"They've declared," she said.

Mason nodded grimly.

"That's no longer pressure," he said. "That's posture."

Kade was already moving—not toward the door, but toward the window, scanning the road.

"That's daylight," he said. "And daylight binds them to process."

By mid-morning, county vehicles arrived again.

This time they didn't hover.

They lined up.

Marked.
Documented.
Intentional.

A camera appeared—official, mounted, unmistakable.

Witnesses gathered faster now.

Ranch trucks parked openly.
Neighbors stood without pretending to have errands.
Someone lifted a phone—not to provoke, just to record.

Carolyn stepped forward.

Not to the gate.

To the edge of the line.

An official approached, credentials visible, posture firm.

"Ms. Ashford," he said. "You've received the declaration."

"Yes," she replied.

"We're proceeding," he said.

Carolyn nodded.

"On what authority?" she asked.

The man gestured broadly.

"Unified jurisdiction," he said.

Carolyn didn't argue.

She reached into her folder and handed him a single page.

"What's this?" he asked.

"A refusal," she said. "Entered into record."

He glanced at it, then back at her.

"You can't refuse jurisdiction," he said.

Carolyn met his eyes.

"I can refuse access," she replied. "And I am."

The man hesitated.

Behind him, the camera whirred softly.

Witnesses watched.

Kade stood still.

The official took a breath.

"Then you're obstructing," he said.

Carolyn didn't flinch.

"Then document it," she said. "Accurately."

Silence followed.

This wasn't the response they'd rehearsed.

The county attorney arrived shortly after.

That, too, was new.

Not a call.
Not a letter.

Presence.

She stepped out of her vehicle and approached with purpose.

"Ms. Ashford," she said. "We're asserting jurisdiction."

Carolyn nodded.

"And I'm asserting standing," she replied.

The attorney smiled faintly.

"This will escalate," she said.

"Yes," Carolyn replied. "That's what declarations do."

A pause.

"You understand the consequences," the attorney said.

Carolyn's voice remained steady.

"I understand the cost of pretending there aren't any," she said.

The attorney glanced at the watchers.

At the camera.

At the land.

She made a decision.

"We'll seek formal remedy," she said.

Carolyn inclined her head.

"Please do," she replied.

By afternoon, the declaration was already being parsed.

Legal blogs.
Local radio.

County statements walking back tone without retracting language.

Too late.

They'd stepped into daylight.

"They can't unsay it," Mason said later. "Now they have to defend it."

"Yes," Carolyn replied.

Kade leaned against the counter, finally allowing himself to speak more than a sentence.

"They wanted inevitability," he said. "They got visibility."

Carolyn closed the laptop.

"And visibility has rules," she said.

That evening, the property was quiet again.

But it wasn't the old quiet.

It was the quiet after something has been named.

Carolyn stood at the window, watching the last light fall across the line that hadn't moved despite every attempt to redraw it.

Behind her, Kade spoke softly.

"They'll come back," he said. "But not like before."

She nodded.

"They can't," she said. "They've declared."

Silence stretched.

Then, without looking at him, she spoke—quiet, controlled.

"Thank you," she said.

"For what?" he asked.

"For standing where you stood," she replied.

Kade didn't answer right away.

"Anytime," he said finally.

But they both knew that wasn't what he meant.

By nightfall, filings were being drafted.

Positions hardened.

Lines named.

Act II was complete.

The system had spoken.

And now, the cost of being visible would be paid—by everyone.

Chapter 21

THE HOLD

The morning after the declaration felt deceptively normal.

No vehicles.
No notices.
No watchers lingering on the road.

That was the first test.

Carolyn noticed it immediately—not as relief, but as recalibration.

"They're letting it breathe," Mason said when he arrived. "Giving it room to settle."

"Yes," Carolyn replied. "So they can claim stability."

Kade stood by the window, eyes tracking the empty road.

"They're shifting to duration," he said. "They want to see who gets tired first."

The county's filing appeared online before noon.

Clean.
Confident.
Carefully scoped.

A petition for declaratory authority.

Not enforcement.
Not seizure.

Just a request for confirmation that what they'd asserted was already true.

"They're asking the court to bless the declaration," Mason said. "No action yet. Just legitimacy."

Carolyn nodded.

"That's safer for them," she said. "They're betting the process favors institutions."

Kade spoke quietly.

"It often does," he said. "Unless someone refuses to hurry."

The trust reacted unevenly.

One trustee emailed support—brief, noncommittal, but present.

Another asked for updates twice in one day.

A third went silent.

"They're watching the clock," Mason said.

"Yes," Carolyn replied. "And each other."

Holding wasn't just about the county anymore.

It was about whether anyone else would.

By afternoon, the first call came from outside the usual orbit.

A local attorney.
Not representing anyone.
Just "checking in."

"I saw the filing," he said. "It's... ambitious."

"That's one word for it," Carolyn replied.

"You'll need patience," he added.

Carolyn smiled faintly.

"I have land," she said. "Patience comes with it."

The attorney laughed softly.

"That's what I hoped you'd say," he replied.

When the call ended, she didn't celebrate.

She noted.

The day passed without incident.

That was the second test.

No escalation.
No retreat.

Just waiting.

By evening, the weight returned—not heavier than before, but steadier.

This was endurance now.

Carolyn sat at the table with the petition open, reading not for content but for rhythm.

What they emphasized.
What they avoided.
What they assumed would go unchallenged.

Behind her, Kade remained quiet.

Not because he had nothing to say.

Because he understood when presence was enough.

"They're counting on allowing fatigue to do the work," she said finally.

"Yes," he replied.

"And if it doesn't?"

Kade didn't answer right away.

"Then they'll look for a fracture," he said. "Somewhere they can apply leverage without touching you directly."

Carolyn nodded.

"They already tried that."

"Yes," he said. "They'll try again."

Later, alone, she stepped outside.

The land was dark but familiar, the line invisible yet absolute.

Holding wasn't dramatic.

It didn't feel like resistance.

It felt like **staying**.

Her phone buzzed once.

Friend:
You sound steadier now.

Carolyn paused.

Carolyn:
I am.

A beat.

Friend:
Is that because you figured something out… or because someone's there?

Carolyn looked back at the house, where a single light burned.

Carolyn:
Because I stopped moving.

The friend didn't reply.

She didn't need to.

Inside, Kade stood near the counter, reviewing nothing in particular.

"They'll come back," he said quietly.

"Yes," Carolyn replied.

"But not today," he added.

"No," she agreed.

Today was for holding.

For letting the declaration sit in daylight.

For allowing others to decide whether they were willing to be seen alongside it.

She closed the petition and set it aside.

Act III had begun.

And for the first time, the system wasn't pressing.

It was waiting.

So was she.

Chapter 22

WEIGHT

The court's narrowing order arrived without commentary.

No rebuke.
No validation.

Just boundaries.

Carolyn read it once at her desk, then again standing, then finally folded the page and set it aside as if it were something physical that needed a place.

They had reduced the field.

That mattered.

But reduction came with a cost no filing could measure.

The calls slowed.

Not stopped—slowed.

People who had once checked in casually now waited for permission they didn't ask for. Conversations ended sooner. Invitations became conditional.

No one said why.

They didn't need to.

Holding didn't scare institutions.
It unsettled people.

Carolyn noticed the absences more than the resistance.

A trustee who had once lingered after meetings now gathered his papers early.
A consultant declined to weigh in "until things settled."

Settled.

She let the word pass without comment.

That evening, she walked the property alone.

The land held steady.
The fence line hadn't moved.

Nothing here had changed.

That was the contradiction.

Holding wasn't heavy.

Losing people quietly was.

She stopped there—refused the thought anything further.

Acknowledgment was not indulgence.

At the house, Kade stood near the window, as he often did when the day ended without resolution.

"They'll come back," he said.

"Yes," she replied. "Or they won't."

Either way, the line held.

Inside, Mason left a voicemail she didn't immediately return.

Not avoidance.

Just space.

She needed to feel the shape of the day without commentary.

Later, when she did call him back, her voice was even.

"They're responding," he said.

"Yes," Carolyn replied. "Differently."

"That's a win," he offered.

She paused.

"No," she said. "It's a consequence."

Night settled in cleanly.

No vehicles.
No lights beyond the house.

Carolyn stood at the window—not waiting, not bracing.

Just standing.

Weight wasn't something you carried.

It was something you accepted without explanation.

And once accepted, it stopped asking for attention.

Chapter 23

INTERVENTION

The motion hit the docket just after midnight.

Carolyn read it before sunrise.

Not because she couldn't sleep.

Because she'd learned that escalation rarely announced itself during business hours.

Motion to Intervene
Filed by: *Regional Infrastructure Consortium*

She recognized the name immediately.

They weren't hostile.

They weren't local.

They were patient.

"This isn't the county," Mason said when he arrived. "This is scale."

Carolyn nodded.

"They waited until the question was open," she said. "Now they want standing."

Kade stood at the counter, hands resting lightly on the surface, eyes still.

"They don't intervene to help," he said. "They intervene to position."

The filing was elegant.

No accusations.
No demands.

Just interest.

Material impact.
Operational uncertainty.
Public-private alignment.

They weren't challenging her authority.

They were sidestepping it.

"They're saying the outcome affects them regardless of who holds," Mason said.

"Yes," Carolyn replied. "Which means they don't care who holds—as long as someone predictable does."

Kade nodded.

"And predictable never looks like you," he said.

Carolyn didn't smile.

"That's the price of not being owned," she said.

By mid-morning, the phones woke up.

Calls from law firms she hadn't contacted.
Emails offering "strategic insight."
Messages that praised restraint while hinting at alternatives.

The language was consistent.

Resolution.
Stability.
Forward momentum.

They wanted movement.

Any movement.

Holding was starting to look inconvenient.

The county responded within hours.

Not publicly.

Procedurally.

They didn't oppose the intervention.

They welcomed it.

"That tells you everything," Mason said.

"Yes," Carolyn replied. "They want distance."

Distance created deniability.

If the outcome went badly, it wouldn't be *them*.

That afternoon, the first reporter showed up.

Not aggressive.

Not dramatic.

Just curious.

"I'm trying to understand what this is really about," she said.

Carolyn considered her carefully.

"It's about who decides when silence becomes consent," she said.

The reporter nodded.

"And you're saying—?"

"I'm saying silence isn't permission," Carolyn replied.

The reporter wrote that down.

That mattered.

Later, when the calls slowed, Carolyn sat alone at the table, the motion open in front of her.

This was the moment she'd anticipated.

Not confrontation.

Crowding.

More actors meant less clarity.

More voices meant more pressure to simplify.

And simplification always favored institutions.

Kade entered quietly and stopped a few steps away.

"They're filling the room," he said.

"Yes," she replied.

"And if it gets crowded enough?" he asked.

"They hope I disappear," she said.

He didn't argue.

"That's often how it works," he said.

The trust convened again that evening.

This time, no one pretended calm.

"This is getting bigger," one trustee said.

"Yes," Carolyn replied.

"And more expensive," another added.

"Yes," she agreed.

A third spoke softly.

"At some point, holding costs more than yielding."

Carolyn looked at him.

"That's true," she said. "If holding is the only thing you're doing."

Silence followed.

She let it.

"This isn't about winning," she continued. "It's about deciding who gets to decide."

No one challenged that.

But not everyone accepted it.

After the meeting, the house felt emptier.

Not physically.

Psychologically.

Kade stood near the door, waiting.

"They're choosing now," he said.

"Yes," she replied.

"And you?" he asked.

Carolyn didn't answer immediately.

"I'm not," she said finally. "I'm holding until they have to."

He nodded once.

"That's the hardest choice," he said.

Later, alone, she reread the motion one last time.

Intervention meant attention.

Attention meant compression.

Time would move again—but faster now.

The system had invited others into the conflict to avoid owning it alone.

That tactic worked.

Until it didn't.

Carolyn closed the file.

Intervention had changed the shape of the field.

Next, someone would try to name it.

And when they did, holding would require more than presence.

It would require declaration—of a different kind.

Chapter 24

NAMING

The first headline appeared before the hearing date was set.

Not inflammatory.
Not wrong.

Just... framed.

County Faces Challenge Over Trust Land Authority

Carolyn read it once and felt the shift immediately.

Challenge.

Not assertion.
Not overreach.

Challenge implied uncertainty on *both* sides.

"They've equalized the positions," Mason said when he saw it. "That's intentional."

"Yes," Carolyn replied. "Language is doing the work now."

Kade stood near the window, arms loose, gaze fixed outward.

"They're naming the conflict in a way that removes origin," he said. "No one started it. It just exists."

By noon, variations followed.

Dispute.
Standoff.
Unclear authority.

Each word shaved something off the edge.

Not truth.

Responsibility.

"They're laundering pressure through vocabulary," Mason said.

Carolyn nodded.

"They're turning a line into a question," she said.

The county's statement came next.

Carefully written.
Heavily vetted.

The county remains committed to collaborative solutions and welcomes judicial clarity regarding governance questions affecting regional stakeholders.

Judicial clarity.

That phrase mattered.

"They want the court to name it," Mason said.

"Yes," Carolyn replied. "So they don't have to."

Kade spoke quietly.

"And courts name things narrowly," he said. "They avoid philosophy."

Carolyn looked at him.

"Then we don't," she said.

The motion to intervene generated its own coverage.

Less local.
More technical.

Analysts speculated.

Commentators debated *efficiency*.

No one talked about legitimacy.

Not yet.

That word made institutions nervous.

That afternoon, a call came from a reporter she hadn't expected.

National outlet.
Measured voice.

"I'm trying to understand the core issue," the reporter said. "Is this about land… or authority?"

Carolyn didn't answer immediately.

She chose her words carefully.

"It's about whether authority is assumed," she said, "or earned through consent."

The reporter paused.

"That's... a sharper distinction," she said.

Carolyn didn't elaborate.

Sharp distinctions tended to cut both ways.

The trust reacted unevenly to the coverage.

One trustee forwarded an article with no comment. Another asked whether messaging should be coordinated. A third suggested silence.

"They want to manage perception," Mason said.

"Yes," Carolyn replied. "Which means perception is now leverage."

Kade nodded.

"And leverage invites naming," he said.

That evening, Carolyn sat alone with a legal pad she still hadn't written on.

Not because she lacked words.

Because choosing the *right* ones mattered now.

Naming wasn't branding.

It wasn't rhetoric.

It was definition.

Define the conflict one way, and authority looked reasonable.

Define it another, and authority looked borrowed.

Her phone buzzed.

Friend:
I heard you on the radio. You sounded... calm.

Carolyn stared at the message.

Carolyn:
Calm isn't the same as neutral.

A moment passed.

Friend:
You're letting them talk around you.

Carolyn set the phone down.

She was letting them exhaust the wrong words.

Kade joined her quietly.

"They'll try to name you next," he said.

"Yes," she replied.

"As stubborn," he added. "Or ideological."

She nodded.

"That's what happens when you don't volunteer language," she said.

He studied her.

"Do you know what you'll say when you do?" he asked.

Carolyn looked at the blank page.

"Yes," she said.

"But not yet."

He accepted that.

Late that night, a longer piece ran online.

More thoughtful.

Less cautious.

It used a new phrase.

The Claim.

Carolyn read it twice.

Not because it flattered her.

Because it clarified something essential.

Claims weren't just about land.

They were about **who believed they had the right to speak first**.

She closed the laptop.

Naming had begun.

Soon, she would have to answer—not by arguing the county's words...

...but by choosing her own.

Chapter 25

THE STATEMENT

The statement was shorter than everyone expected.

That was intentional.

Carolyn released it mid-morning—not early enough to look defensive, not late enough to look reactive.

No press conference.
No podium.
No backdrop.

Just text.

It appeared on the trust's site, timestamped and unembellished.

Statement from the Ashford Trust

The Ashford Trust has not challenged the authority of the county.

It has declined to surrender authority that was never granted.

This matter is not about access, development, or obstruction.
It is about whether jurisdiction can be assumed without consent—and whether silence is treated as agreement.

The Trust will continue to hold its responsibilities as written, without escalation and without retreat.

Any clarification sought by the court is welcome.

Any action taken without consent is not.

That was it.

No adjectives.
No accusations.
No appeal.

Just definition.

Mason read it twice.

"They can't argue with this," he said. "Not directly."

"No," Carolyn replied. "They have to talk around it."

Kade stood quietly near the counter.

"And talking around something," he said, "means it's already landed."

The reaction was immediate—but uneven.

Local radio read it verbatim.
A regional paper quoted the second paragraph in full.
Online commentary split cleanly—some calling it firm, others calling it evasive.

The county responded within hours.

Not angrily.

Cautiously.

The county respects the Trust's position and looks forward to judicial guidance on shared governance concerns.

Shared.

Governance.

Concerns.

They were still trying to blur the line.

"They're avoiding the word consent," Mason said.

"Yes," Carolyn replied. "Because they can't accept it without narrowing themselves."

Kade nodded.

"They want authority to remain ambient," he said. "Unspoken. Automatic."

Carolyn closed her laptop.

"Then it stays named," she said.

The trust's inbox filled by afternoon.

Messages from people she didn't know.

Some supportive.
Some anxious.
Some carefully neutral.

One stood out.

A short note from a landowner two counties over.

Thank you for saying what the rest of us don't know how to say yet.

Carolyn read it once.

She didn't reply.

But she kept it.

By evening, the motion to intervene had drawn responses.

Some opposing.
Some aligning.

The case was no longer narrow.

It was becoming illustrative.

"They didn't want this," Mason said. "They wanted resolution without precedent."

Carolyn nodded.

"And now?" he asked.

"And now it's precedent-adjacent," she said. "Which makes everyone nervous."

Kade added quietly.

"And careful."

That night, Carolyn stood alone at the window longer than usual.

The statement hadn't lightened anything.

It had clarified.

Clarity carried weight.

Her phone buzzed.

Friend:
I read it.

Carolyn waited.

Friend:
That was... very you.

A pause.

Friend:
Are you okay with what comes next?

Carolyn considered the question.

Not emotionally.

Strategically.

Carolyn:
I'm okay with what it means.

The friend didn't respond immediately.

When she did, it was only one line.

Friend:
Then you're ready.

Behind her, footsteps approached.

Kade stopped a respectful distance away.

"They heard you," he said.

"Yes," Carolyn replied.

"And they'll respond," he added.

"Yes."

Silence followed—not heavy, not tense.

Just settled.

"They'll try to make you loud next," he said.

Carolyn shook her head.

"I don't need to be loud," she said. "I've already been clear."

He smiled faintly.

"That's worse for them," he said.

Outside, the land remained unchanged.

Inside the system, something had shifted.

The conflict had been named.

Not as dispute.
Not as misunderstanding.

But as a question of consent.

And questions like that didn't resolve quietly.

They either disappeared...

...or they restructured the room.

Chapter 26

RESPONSE

The response didn't come as a rebuttal.

That would have elevated her.

Instead, it came as motion.

At 10:14 a.m., the county filed an amended petition.

Not longer.
Not louder.

Broader.

Carolyn saw it within minutes.

"They didn't contest the statement," Mason said, scanning the document. "They widened the frame."

"Yes," Carolyn replied. "They're trying to drown the definition."

Kade stood nearby, already reading the posture rather than the words.

"They're converting a consent question into an administrative necessity," he said.

The amended filing replaced specificity with scope.

Regional coordination.
Operational continuity.
Public interest.

Nothing about her.
Nothing about the trust.

Just inevitability.

By noon, the county vehicles returned—not to the property, but to town.

Permits paused.
Inspections delayed.
Appointments "rescheduled."

No declarations.

Just friction—now officially normalized.

"They're responding by reasserting tempo," Mason said. "Trying to prove they control time."

"Yes," Carolyn replied. "Because they lost control of language."

Kade nodded.

"And time feels safer," he said. "Until it doesn't."

The first real counterweight appeared unexpectedly.

A clerk from the court called Mason—not Carolyn.

Procedural. Polite.

"There will be a scheduling conference," she said. "Sooner rather than later."

Mason covered the receiver and looked up.

"They don't like the ambiguity," he said. "Judges don't."

Carolyn nodded.

"That's the cost of widening," she said. "It invites containment."

The afternoon news cycle noticed the shift.

Not the filing.

The **behavior**.

A local columnist wrote:

The county's answer to a question about consent appears to be expansion.

Carolyn read that line twice.

Kade noticed.

"They saw it," he said.

"Yes," she replied. "Someone always does."

Late in the day, the trust received a formal notice from a contractor.

They were withdrawing—politely, regretfully, permanently.

Not because of money.

Because of "uncertainty."

The word carried weight now.

Carolyn closed the email and set it aside.

"That's the price," Mason said quietly.

"Yes," she replied. "And it's visible."

Kade spoke carefully.

"They're trying to make holding lonely," he said.

Carolyn looked at him.

"It was always lonely," she said. "Now it's just obvious."

That evening, a second message arrived—from a source she hadn't expected.

A regional association of land trusts.

Short. Direct.

We read your statement.
If this proceeds, we may submit an amicus.

Carolyn didn't move for several seconds.

Mason exhaled slowly.

"That changes things," he said.

"Yes," Carolyn replied. "Because now it's not just mine."

Kade nodded.

"And they can't widen forever," he said. "At some point, breadth becomes exposure."

Night settled in without ceremony.

No vehicles.
No calls.

But something had shifted again.

The system had responded—not by disproving her definition...

...but by trying to outgrow it.

That tactic worked until it didn't.

Carolyn stood at the window one last time.

The land was quiet.

The case was not.

She understood now what response really meant.

Not rebuttal.

Commitment.

They had committed—to action, to scope, to daylight.

And commitment could be measured.

Tomorrow, the court would set time.

And time, finally, would stop being theirs.

Chapter 27

CONTAINMENT

The court didn't move quickly.

It moved **precisely**.

The scheduling order posted at 8:41 a.m.—no fanfare, no explanation.

Just boundaries.

A hearing date.
A limited scope.
A directive for briefing confined to **standing and consent**.

Carolyn read it once.

Then again.

"They narrowed it," Mason said, already smiling despite himself. "They cut away everything else."

"Yes," Carolyn replied. "They contained it."

Kade stood near the window, watching the road like he always did when something fundamental shifted.

"Courts don't like sprawl," he said. "It makes decisions slippery."

"And slippery decisions create appeals," Mason added.

Carolyn closed the laptop.

"They've forced the system to answer the question it tried to avoid," she said.

The county's reaction came faster than expected.

Not public.

Internal.

Emails began circulating—she saw them because someone forwarded one with no note attached.

We need to recalibrate.
This is narrower than anticipated.
Exposure risk increasing.

They were discovering what containment felt like from the inside.

"They wanted breadth," Mason said. "They got a box."

"Yes," Carolyn replied. "And boxes demand precision."

Kade nodded.

"And precision demands ownership," he said. "Someone has to stand behind it."

By noon, the motion to intervene was addressed.

Not denied.

Deferred.

The court wanted to know whether third parties were even necessary **before** standing was resolved.

"That's a polite 'not yet,'" Mason said.

"Yes," Carolyn replied. "Which is worse than no."

Kade allowed himself a faint smile.

"They're being told to wait," he said. "Institutions hate that."

The media noticed the shift—but didn't understand it yet.

Headlines softened.

Judge Sets Parameters in County–Trust Dispute
Key Question Narrowed Ahead of Hearing

The word *narrowed* appeared twice.

That was enough.

"They lost momentum," Mason said.

"No," Carolyn corrected. "They lost diffusion."

She stood and walked to the window, looking out at the land that had been the pretext for everything—and yet had never changed.

"Now it's about what they can defend," she said. "Not what they can imply."

The afternoon passed quietly.

No vehicles.
No calls.

The quiet wasn't strategic this time.

It was procedural.

Everyone was preparing.

Carolyn felt the shift physically—not relief, but **load redistribution**.

Pressure was no longer pressing outward.

It was compressing inward.

That changed who could bear it.

Late in the day, Mason received a call from a colleague at the county.

Off the record.
Careful.

"They're arguing internally," Mason said after hanging up. "About who authorized the declaration."

Carolyn nodded.

"That always happens once containment sets in," she said.

Kade added quietly.

"When daylight hits process, blame looks for shelter."

That evening, as the light faded, Carolyn stood on the porch again.

Not because she needed to.

Because she always did.

Kade joined her, stopping a few feet away.

"They can't widen anymore," he said.

"No," she replied. "They have to justify."

"And justification," he continued, "creates fingerprints."

Carolyn nodded.

"That's what they were trying to avoid from the beginning."

Silence settled between them—calm, steady, unforced.

For the first time since the declaration, the stillness felt different.

Not like waiting.

Like alignment.

Inside, her phone buzzed.

Friend:
Sounds like the judge just made everyone behave.

Carolyn smiled faintly.

Carolyn:
Judges don't make people behave.
They make them choose.

A pause.

Friend:
And you?

Carolyn looked out at the line one more time.

Carolyn:
I already did.

Containment had done its work.

The field was smaller now.

Sharper.

And in a smaller field, holding didn't just require endurance.

It required **clarity**.

Next, the system would have to decide whether it could defend what it had claimed—without hiding behind momentum.

And that decision would not be quiet.

Chapter 28

STANDING

The hearing room was smaller than Carolyn expected.

That was intentional.

No gallery.
No cameras.
No flags.

Just a judge, a clerk, and two tables facing each other like this was an argument that should never have needed witnesses.

Carolyn sat at the left table with Mason.

Kade sat behind her—not close enough to signal alliance, not far enough to disappear.

Present.
Unremarkable.
Steady.

The county's counsel arrived with two associates and a stack of binders that looked heavier than necessary.

Over-preparedness was a tell.

The judge entered without ceremony.

No preliminaries.

No speeches.

"We're here to determine standing," she said. "Not to rehearse grievances."

Good.

Carolyn felt her shoulders settle.

Standing was clean.

Standing was binary.

The county went first.

Their argument was smooth, practiced, and incomplete.

They spoke of:

- regional coordination
- statutory authority
- operational necessity
- public interest

They avoided names.

They avoided consent.

They spoke as if authority existed **because it always had**.

Carolyn listened without reacting.

She wasn't the audience.

The judge was.

And judges listened for what wasn't said.

When it was her turn, Mason stood briefly—only long enough to introduce her.

Then he sat.

Carolyn stood alone.

Not dramatically.

Not defiantly.

Just… upright.

"Your Honor," she said, "this case isn't about what the county may do."

The judge looked up.

"It's about what it may assume."

Silence.

Carolyn continued.

"The county has authority where it is granted. It has jurisdiction where it is defined.

What it does not have is consent—unless silence is treated as agreement."

The judge's pen paused.

Carolyn didn't rush.

"The Trust did not challenge authority.
It declined to surrender it.
That distinction matters."

She stopped there.

Not because she was finished.

Because she knew when to let the weight land.

The county's rebuttal was shorter than planned.

They emphasized precedent.
They cited necessity.
They referenced continuity.

They avoided Carolyn directly.

That avoidance spoke louder than argument.

The judge leaned back.

"Standing," she said slowly, "requires clarity."

Both tables went still.

"Either authority exists independently," the judge continued, "or it is conditioned."

She looked at the county.

"Which is it?"

The county attorney hesitated.

Just a fraction.

But enough.

"We believe," she said carefully, "that authority is implicit."

The judge nodded once.

"Belief," she said, "is not jurisdiction."

The room changed.

Not dramatically.

Decisively.

The judge didn't rule immediately.

She didn't need to.

"I'll issue an order," she said. "Narrow. Specific. Prompt."

She stood.

"This court will not expand authority by assumption," she added. "If the county wishes to assert standing, it must show where it was granted."

Then she left.

Outside the courtroom, the hallway felt wider than it had any right to.

Mason exhaled for the first time in hours.

"That went... well," he said.

Carolyn nodded.

"It went honestly," she replied.

Kade stepped closer—not touching, not intruding.

"They had to answer," he said. "And they didn't like the answer."

"No," she agreed. "They never do."

The county's team exited without comment.

No posturing.

No smiles.

Just recalculation.

Containment had done its final work.

Standing had been named.

And authority—once assumed—was now exposed to daylight.

Later that evening, back at the property, Carolyn stood at the window again.

Not waiting.

Just acknowledging where she was.

Kade stood nearby, quiet as ever.

"They'll comply," he said. "Or appeal."

"Yes," she replied.

"And either way?" he asked.

She looked out at the land—the same line, unchanged.

"Either way," she said, "they can't pretend anymore."

Silence settled.

Not the tense silence of pressure.

The clean silence of something decided.

Her phone buzzed.

Friend:
Did it happen?

Carolyn smiled faintly.

Carolyn:
Yes.

A pause.

Friend:
And you?

Carolyn glanced once at Kade—only long enough to register steadiness.

Carolyn:
Still standing.

Standing wasn't victory.

It wasn't closure.

It was recognition.

And recognition, once granted, was hard to revoke.

The system had finally been forced to say what it believed.

Now it would have to live with it.

Chapter 29

AFTERMATH

The order posted two days later.

Not dramatic.
Not sweeping.
Just unmistakable.

The court declined to recognize county standing absent explicit grant or consent.
Field actions were stayed.
Jurisdictional assumptions were cautioned against pending further showing.

No rebuke.
No lecture.
Just limits.

Carolyn read it once, then again—not for validation, but for secondary effects.

Aftermath never lived in the ruling itself.
It lived in what people did next.

The county's response was immediate—and uneven.

One department quietly resumed delayed permits.
Another froze communications entirely.
A third requested a "clarifying meeting" that no one scheduled.

"They're re-sorting internally," Mason said. "Trying to figure out what still works."

"Yes," Carolyn replied. "And who owns what no longer does."

Kade listened, arms folded loosely.

"Authority doesn't disappear," he said. "It migrates."

Carolyn nodded.
"And migration leaves tracks."

By early November, the media tone had softened.

Not supportive.
Respectful.

Headlines shifted language rather than posture.

Judge Questions County Standing
Trust Authority Recognized Pending Consent

Recognized.

The word mattered. It suggested legitimacy without celebration. Existence without endorsement.

"This is the best kind of coverage," Mason said. "Boring to outsiders. Alarming to insiders."

Carolyn allowed herself a faint smile.

"Yes," she said. "Because nothing unsettles institutions like precedent that doesn't shout."

The trust felt the ruling unevenly.

One trustee called immediately—relieved, almost buoyant.
Another sent a short message:

I still think this could've been avoided.

Carolyn didn't respond.

Avoided was a word people used when they hadn't carried the weight.

That afternoon, the first unsolicited visit arrived.

A county official—not enforcement, not legal.
Planning.

He stood at the edge of the drive, hands visible, posture careful.

"I'm here to listen," he said.

Carolyn stepped outside.

"That's new," she replied.

"Yes," he agreed. "We're… reassessing."

She nodded.

"Then start by understanding consent," she said.

He didn't argue.

That was new too.

Inside, later, the house felt different.

Not lighter.
Quieter in a way that wasn't braced.

Kade leaned against the counter, finally letting a full breath leave him.

"They didn't lose," he said.

"No," Carolyn replied. "They learned."

"And learning hurts."

"Yes," she said. "Which is why they resist it."

That night, Carolyn sat alone longer than usual.

The adrenaline was gone.
What remained was clarity—and a subtle cost she hadn't named yet.

Winning standing didn't end conflict.
It redistributed it.

People who had relied on ambient authority would now have to ask.
People who had benefited from silence would now have to speak.

And some would resent her for it.

That was the real aftermath.

Her phone buzzed.

Friend:
So… what now?

Carolyn considered the question.
Not strategically.
Personally.

Carolyn:
Now everyone has to be honest about what they're doing.

A pause.

Friend:
That sounds exhausting.

Carolyn smiled to herself.

Carolyn:
Only for people who weren't already.

Kade appeared in the doorway—not interrupting, just present.

"They'll come back," he said. "Later. Differently."

"Yes."

"But not like before."

"No," she agreed. "They can't."

They stood in the quiet together.

No celebration.
No relief parade.

Just the shared understanding that something had shifted—and couldn't be reset.

Aftermath wasn't loud.

It was structural.

And structures, once altered, never quite returned to their original shape.

Chapter 30

RECORD

The filing appeared on a Thursday.

Not announced.
Not flagged.
Just entered.

Carolyn found it because she knew where to look—not for conflict, but for permanence.

A memorandum of acknowledgment.
Recorded.
Indexed.
Public.

It did not assign blame.
It did not resolve jurisdiction.

It did something quieter.

It stated—without argument—that the Ashford Trust did not consent to county authority absent explicit statutory grant, and that any future engagement would require written acknowledgment of that limit.

No flourish.
No legal theater.

Just a line entered into a system designed to remember.

Mason read it twice before speaking.

"They won't like this."

"No," Carolyn replied. "They won't be able to ignore it."

"That's different."

"Yes," she agreed. "That's the point."

Once something was recorded, it stopped being negotiable in the dark.

The county's response was careful.

No appeal.
No rebuttal.

Just a brief internal notice, circulated and re-circulated, advising departments to *observe recorded limitations pending further guidance.*

Observe.

Carolyn smiled faintly.

Observation was the language of restraint.

By the following week, the visits stopped entirely.

So did the calls.

Not because the issue was resolved—but because the path around it had narrowed.

Precedent had weight.
And weight traveled.

Carolyn walked the property one last time before the season turned.

Not to check boundaries.
Not to reassure herself.

Just to be present.

Kade followed at a distance—not guarding, not guiding.

Witnessing.

"They'll take this higher," he said.

"Yes."

"And when they do?"

She stopped at the line.

"Then it won't be about land," she said. "It'll be about whether systems can admit limits once they've been recorded."

He considered that.

"That's a harder question."

"Yes," she agreed. "Which is why it won't stay here."

That night, Carolyn drafted one final letter.

Not to the county.
Not to counsel.

To the trustees.

Short. Direct.

The Trust has been recognized in record.
This chapter is complete.
What follows will not be local, and it will not be quiet.
I will remain until transition is complete, then step back.

No vote requested.
No permission sought.

Holding did not require consensus.

Her phone buzzed once, late.

Friend:
So… is it over?

Carolyn stood at the window, the land dark and unchanged beyond the glass.

Carolyn:
This part is.

A pause.

Friend:
And you?

Carolyn didn't answer immediately.

She thought of the cost.
The clarity.
The record.

Then she typed.

Carolyn:
I did what I came to do.

The house settled into its old sounds.

Wind.
Wood.
Distance.

Carolyn turned off the light and stood in the dark a moment longer than necessary.

Not waiting.

Just acknowledging.

The system had tested restraint and mistaken it for weakness.

Now it had a record to contend with.

And records, once entered, did not argue.

They endured.

Chapter 31

DEPARTURE

The idea came easily.

They were standing near the hangar as the light softened, the day already slipping toward evening. Maggie lay stretched out on the concrete, chin on her paws, watching nothing in particular.

Carolyn mentioned the Gulfstream almost as an aside—family logistics, availability, the familiar language of money solving inconvenience.

Kade shook his head once. Not dismissive. Just practical.

"I'm headed east anyway," he said. "No reason to make a thing of it."

She looked at him.

"I can drop you," he added. "It's not out of my way."

There was no pause after that.
No recalculation.

The answer had arrived fully formed.

They flew the next morning.

The PC-24 sat ready, quiet and purposeful. Frost edged the ramp. Maggie climbed aboard first, tail wagging once before settling in as if she'd already decided where she belonged.

Carolyn hesitated only a moment before taking the right seat.

She wasn't used to being forward.
Used to space behind curtains.
To being carried rather than involved.

Now she was beside him, headset on, watching as Kade moved through his checks with calm precision.

Not hurried.
Not showy.

Correct.

This wasn't the man she'd seen leaning against a truck or standing quietly in doorways.

This was Kade at work.

Pilot.
Fixer.
Professional.

Someone you trusted because he didn't need you to notice him doing his job.

The PC-24 lifted cleanly, Wyoming falling away beneath them as distance flattened the land. Maggie shifted once, then settled.

The cabin was quiet—not heavy. Not awkward.

They didn't talk about the case.
There was nothing left to process.

They talked about ordinary things.

Holiday travel.
How winter slowed Wyoming to a crawl.
How nothing important moved there after Thanksgiving anyway.

"Home's a good place to regroup," Kade said, eyes forward. "Especially when nothing's asking for your attention."

Carolyn nodded.

She understood now why her father had loved this place. Why he'd chosen stillness when the world kept offering motion.

They landed smoothly.

Carolyn set the headset carefully in the right seat before stepping down from the cabin, leaving it exactly where it had been.

At the curb, she paused with her bag in hand.

"Thank you," she said.

It wasn't just for the flight.

Kade nodded. "Anytime."

Maggie watched from the cabin, tail thumping once.

Carolyn turned toward the terminal without looking back. She didn't need to. Some things didn't require watching to know they were still there.

Kade waited until she was inside before bringing the engines back to life.

The PC-24 turned west, then south, climbing steadily into the late-day sky. The sun hung low, throwing long light across the horizon.

His flight plan was already set.

Key West.

Nothing urgent.
Nothing unfinished.

Maggie moved up front and settled into the right seat as if it had always been hers.

The aircraft leveled off.

Behind him, winter would settle in.
Ahead, the light was still good.

Kade trimmed the aircraft and let it run, the sun lowering slowly as they flew on—no destination that needed explaining, no story that needed telling.

Just motion.

Just space.

And enough sky to leave the rest to imagination.

END OF BOOK TWO — *THE CLAIM*

About the Author

Kevin Seney is a pilot, licensed investigator, and lifelong storyteller whose fiction is rooted in the American West—where land remembers, power moves quietly, and loyalty still matters. Drawing on a background in business intelligence and years spent navigating high-stakes environments, his stories explore what happens when people are forced to choose between inheritance and integrity.

A former CEO, Seney now writes full time, crafting modern Western narratives that blend restraint, consequence, and emotional depth. His work favors quiet tension over spectacle, relationships over rhetoric, and the kind of truth that doesn't announce itself—until it can no longer be ignored.

He lives in Park City, Utah, with his wife Carrie, their six daughters, and two German Shorthaired Pointers—Maggie and Aspen.

"Stories about land, legacy, and the cost of staying."

The Ashford Line

A Modern Western Saga

Power doesn't always arrive loud.
Sometimes it waits.

When a legacy ranch in northern Wyoming becomes the quiet center of an emerging land war, the fight isn't about ownership—it's about precedent. About who gets to decide what stays whole, what gets divided, and what history is allowed to disappear.

At the center stands Carolyn Ashford, a woman who inherits more than land. She inherits pressure. Memory. And a choice no one else wants to make.

Alongside her is Kade Vance—pilot, investigator, and fixer—drawn into a conflict where authority wears clean boots, process becomes a weapon, and restraint is mistaken for weakness. Together, they navigate a world where deals are made without signatures, retaliation arrives sideways, and staying is the most dangerous move of all.

Book One — *The Forge*
A legacy is tested.
A trust is formed.
And the first lines are drawn.

This is not a story about winning.
It's a story about holding.

For readers who love the grounded intensity of *Taylor Sheridan*, the moral gravity of *Craig Johnson*, and character-driven modern Westerns where land remembers and power moves quietly, **The Ashford Line** is a slow-burn saga about inheritance, alignment, and the cost of staying long enough to matter.

Because in Wyoming, the land doesn't forget.

And it doesn't forgive lightly.

Made in the USA
Coppell, TX
23 January 2026

69098144R00156